THE HAUNTING OF HOOVER DAM

THE MYSTERY HOUSE SERIES, BOOK FIVE

Eva Pohler

Copyright © 2019 by Eva Pohler.

All rights reserved. No part of this publication may be reproduced, distributed or transmitted in any form or by any means, including photocopying, recording, or other electronic or mechanical methods, without the prior written permission of the publisher, except in the case of brief quotations embodied in critical reviews and certain other noncommercial uses permitted by copyright law. For permission requests, write to the publisher, addressed "Attention: Permissions Coordinator," at the address below.

Eva Pohler Books
20011 Park Ranch
San Antonio, Texas 78259
www.evapohler.com

Publisher's Note: This is a work of fiction. Names, characters, places, and incidents are a product of the author's imagination. Locales and public names are sometimes used for atmospheric purposes. Any resemblance to actual people, living or dead, or to businesses, companies, events, institutions, or locales is completely coincidental.

Book Layout ©2017 BookDesignTemplates.com

Book Cover Design by Keri Knutson

The Haunting of Hoover Dam/ Eva Pohler. -- 1st ed.
Paperback ISBN 978-1-958390-28-3

Contents

For the Hoover Dam workers who "died to make the desert bloom" but weren't acknowledged.

A Rough Start

I don't know," Tanya said from where she sat beside Ellen and across from Sue, in their usual booth at Panera.

The window beside Ellen was hotter than her black bean soup, due to the relentless rays of the August sun, which perched at high noon.

"I think we should wait at least one more month," Tanya said.

Tanya glanced at each of them with her troubled blue eyes before fidgeting with her salad. Her long blonde hair had been pulled back into a ponytail at the nape of her neck, giving Ellen, beside her, a full view of Tanya's frown. It seemed to Ellen that Tanya thought the subject was now closed.

Ellen took a sip of her iced tea and hid her exasperation. "Every doctor in Boulder City has said the same thing: It's not contagious. They think the symptoms are psychosomatic. No actual flu virus has been detected."

"I'm not sure I'm ready to risk my life on the word of five or six Podunk doctors," Sue said before taking a bite of her broccoli cheddar soup.

Ellen bit her lip. She'd hoped to have Sue on her side, but she'd forgotten what a hypochondriac her friend was. Ellen supposed she should be glad that Sue hadn't believed she'd *already come down* with the Phantom Flu.

"No one's *died* from it, Sue. And Boulder City is not a Podunk town," Ellen argued. "It's just a hop, a skip, and a jump away from Las Vegas. Now that they're saying it's psychosomatic, the quarantine has been lifted. It's not the bird flu, or the swine flu, or viral pneumonia. It's not bacterial, either. They're calling it the Phantom Flu for *a reason*."

"Look who's calling the kettle black," Sue complained as she brushed her dark bangs from her eyes.

Ellen furrowed her brows. "I didn't call anybody anything."

"No," Tanya said. "But you're frustrated with us for being skeptics when that's usually *your* M.O."

Tanya crossed one long, thin leg over the other, nearly curling into a ball, like a baby giraffe. She continued to frown as she used her fork to scoot salad from one side of her plate to the other.

Ellen sighed. "If the Phantom Flu were the only strange thing going on in Boulder City, I might be convinced that it was caused by an unknown virus that the doctors have been unable to isolate. I might even believe the apparently popular theory that—what are the numbers now? Five hundred and fifty-two?"

Sue nodded.

"I might believe that it's possible for five hundred and fifty-two people to be suffering from mass hysteria. But I truly believe all the evidence points to a significant paranormal event."

Back in May, Tanya and Sue had been chomping at the bit to go. Ellen had wanted to take some time to find closure with Paul. She'd continued to feel guilty about her relationship with Brian. But shortly after Sue and Tanya had convinced Ellen to investigate the strange happenings in Boulder City, news of the flu-like epidemic had swept the nation, and they'd decided to wait.

"Let's just give it until the end of September," Sue said. "The weather will be nicer."

"I'm not waiting," Ellen said.

Tanya and Sue looked up from their plates with their mouths hanging open.

"I'll go by myself, if I have to," Ellen added. "Maybe I'll ask Brian to join me."

"I thought you were going to end things with him," Tanya said before taking a bite of her salad.

"I changed my mind," Ellen said. "And *you're* changing the subject."

"You're bluffing," Sue said, pointing a finger at Ellen. "You won't go without us."

"Maybe I *am* bluffing, and maybe I'm *not*. I want to investigate, to embark on a new adventure. Of course, if I had my choice, I'd rather it be *with* you than *without* you."

Tanya frowned again. "What if the Phantom Flu is caused by spirit attachments—or, worse, possessions? I'm scared, Ellen."

"We have protection against that now." Ellen pinched the *gris gris* bag hanging around her neck beneath her summer blouse.

"Not one-hundred-percent *foolproof* protection," Sue said.

Ellen shot a warning look across the table at Sue. It was a wonder that Tanya had helped in Portland, after enduring a spirit attachment in New Orleans. Did Sue want to deter their friend from ever working with ghosts again?

Ellen folded her napkin onto her plate, having finished the last of her panini. She felt a hot flash coming on as sweat formed on her forehead and dripped down the back of her neck. She wished she'd worn her hair up. Tanya had had the right idea with her ponytail. She wondered how Sue's dark brown hair, which fell to her shoulders, always looked so flawless.

"Come on, guys," Ellen said. "People are suffering and in need of our help. You said so yourself, Sue. The comments on your blog are absolutely heart-wrenching."

Ellen pulled out her phone and went to Sue's blog. Over sixty comments—though some from the same people—were listed on Sue's most recent post. The post had been about the Raven and Rose in Portland, but the comments were all about Boulder City. One man named Carl seemed quite sure that the devil had mistaken Boulder City for Vegas and, after being denied an investigation by the Catholic Church, Carl had come to Sue's blog as a last resort. Another man commented that he would pay Ghost Healers a hundred thousand dollars to investigate.

Ellen found the comment she'd been looking for and read aloud:

"'Please help. My twenty-year-old daughter has been having visions of a man standing over her bed every night since April. Deprived of sleep, Erin missed a lot of work and was fired last Tuesday. Since then, her health has declined, and nothing seems to help. We need you in Boulder City, Nevada!' signed, Mary Jane McGinty."

Sue sighed. "Ellen, I've read my blog. I know what it says."

"Mary Jane has commented with three other pleas for help since then," Ellen said as she scrolled through the comments. "Oh, my gosh. There's a new comment today from someone else. Have you read it yet?"

"No." Sue leaned forward. "What does it say?"

Ellen read, "'As my husband and I were driving home to Boulder City from a weekend getaway in Las Vegas last Sunday night, we saw a young man walking on the side of the road coming into town. He was dragging his feet and stumbling in our headlights. My husband slowed the car as we approached him. The man fell into the middle of the road! My husband stopped the car, and we both ran out to check on him, but the man had disappeared! Meanwhile, another car traveling in the same direction as us nearly killed us. Imagine our horror when we arrived in Boulder City and shared our story with friends, only to discover that at least five other people had seen the same thing. One of them hadn't been as lucky as us. My sister's father-in-law had been run over by another driver the previous night while trying to help what must have been a ghost! Please come to Boulder City and help us!'—signed, Pat Blake."

"That gave me chills," Tanya muttered.

"When did it become our job to save people from ghosts?" Sue asked. "I don't understand why people expect *us* to do something about it."

"*You're* the one who wrote the blog that made us famous," Ellen pointed out. "*You're* the one that made Ghost Healers, Inc. a household name." Then, in a teasing tone, she added, "And, you know the old saying: *With great power comes great responsibility.*"

"Really?" Tanya shook her head before taking another sip of her tea.

Sue sighed. "It may sound cheesy, but Ellen's right."

Tanya looked up at Sue with her brows lifted and her lips parted in surprise. "I thought you were on *my* side."

"We have a gift," Sue said. "And it's our duty to use it for good."

"Even at our own peril?" Tanya asked. "You really want to risk catching this Phantom Flu?"

"No one has died from it," Ellen said again.

"Not *yet*," Tanya said. "And even so, do you really want to suffer with flu-like symptoms indefinitely? They're saying no one's recovered from it, either. It's been months. And we don't know that it won't eventually kill them. Why chance it?"

Sue turned to Ellen. "I'll go with you. When do you want to leave?"

"Why not this weekend?" Ellen suggested.

"I'll check with Tom and let you know."

"Seriously?" Tanya objected. "You'll go without me?"

"If we must," Ellen said.

"Though we'd rather not," Sue added.

Tanya shook her head. "Don't you think you're becoming addicted to this paranormal stuff? If you're willing to risk your health—and even your life—to chase after some ghosts, it might be time to see a therapist."

Ellen folded her hands and turned to Tanya. "You were just as excited about Ghost Healers, Inc. as we were, Tanya. You agreed that we felt called to a higher purpose. I think you still haven't completely recovered from that spirit attachment. Maybe you're the one who needs therapy. And I say that with love."

"I don't need therapy," Tanya insisted.

"None of us needs therapy," Sue said. "And no one's forcing you to go to Boulder City, Tanya. Stay if you want."

"Or come," Ellen added.

"Fine," Tanya huffed. "I'll check with Dave. But if I get sick or die—or worse, get possessed—it's your fault," she added, glaring first at Ellen and then at Sue.

Ellen would be more than happy to take the blame—though she wasn't quite sure how that would help matters. "Great. Text me once you've checked with your husbands."

As they left Panera, Ellen felt a thrill run down her back. It was exciting to be starting something new, even if it was a bit terrifying.

Sunday afternoon, Ellen, Sue, and Tanya sat in a booth at Pappadeaux Seafood Kitchen at the Dallas-Fort Worth airport during a three-hour layover for their connecting flight to Las Vegas. Their flight from San Antonio had been tiring if uneventful. Sue had spent the bulk of the flight convincing them that Pappadeaux was the best place to eat lunch at DFW, even if it was quite a distance from their gate. After a filling lunch, the three hung out in their booth with their carry-on luggage beside them and used their phones to conduct more research on the strange events that had been reportedly taking place in Boulder City since early spring.

"What I want to know is, 'Why now?'" Ellen murmured as she scrolled through another page in her Google search. "Something had to have caused this massive paranormal event, right? Do things like this just randomly and arbitrarily occur? I think not. Wouldn't you agree?"

"According to my research," Tanya began, "the first case of the Phantom Flu was traced back to March 22nd."

"I've not been able to find anything in my research of the Hoover Dam's history that corresponds with March or with this year," Sue said without looking up from her phone. "I was thinking this year might be a significant anniversary, but the dam was built between 1931 and 1936."

"Hold on," Ellen said. "This says that while construction on the dam began in 1931, the preparations began much earlier. Surveyors had begun investigating Boulder Canyon as early as 1921."

Sue smirked. "Well, that might be relevant if this were 2021."

Tanya shook her head. "Do ghosts really care about anniversaries? Are they even aware of them?"

Sue shrugged. "It was just a theory. Why don't you share one of yours? Oh, that's right. You don't have one."

Tanya's face turned red. "I suppose I'll share one when I come up with one worth sharing."

"Now, now." Ellen said. "Sometimes we have to consider the bad ideas in order to come up with the good ones."

Sue furrowed her brows. "I didn't think it was such a bad idea."

"Of course not," Ellen said. "I just meant that we should consider everything, to increase the likelihood of finding the truth."

Sue's look of consternation was immediately replaced by a goofy grin when their handsome waiter approached to see if he could bring them any more water or tea.

It had been an hour since he'd cleared their plates away. Ellen planned to leave the waiter a hefty tip—not because they were keeping him from making money, but because there weren't many tables occupied. It was either a slow day or an unpopular hour for lunch. Ellen had a feeling it was a combination.

Sue had been smitten with their tall, broad-chested waiter, Adrian, since he'd first greeted them. His long dark hair fell to his shoulders, and dark brows contrasted with stunning green eyes. He was probably in his mid-twenties—just a baby—but that didn't stop Sue from smiling up at him with a touch of pink flushing her cheeks.

"Could I get a cherry coke to go?" she asked him as she batted her eyelashes. "I promise to make it worth your while."

Ellen covered her mouth and fought the giggles.

"I meant with a *tip!*" Sue cried, her face reddening.

Adrian laughed with his head thrown back.

"Seriously, guys," Sue scolded, looking like a tomato.

Adrian turned to Ellen and Tanya. "Can I get anything for you, ladies?"

"Nothing for me," Tanya said.

"No, thanks," Ellen added.

"I'll be right back with that cherry coke."

Sue watched the waiter walk away and then turned to Ellen. "Well, I guess I won't be coming to this airport ever again. Thanks a lot, Ellen."

Ellen and Tanya laughed so hard that tears filled their eyes.

When Adrian returned, he handed the coke to Sue, whose fingers trembled with embarrassment as she took the cup.

"Thank you, Adrian," Sue said.

"No worries," he said with a grin. "Hey, didn't I hear you mention that you were waiting on Flight 475 for Las Vegas?"

"Yes," Sue replied. "Why? Are you on that flight, too?"

The look of hope on Sue's face was enough to convince Ellen that her friend had already concocted a fantasy in which Sue and the waiter were seated on the plane, side by side.

"No," he said. "I wish. It's just that I heard them announce last call for boarding passengers. Did you not hear it?"

Ellen, Tanya, and Sue looked at one another with wide eyes.

"No," Sue cried, looking at her phone. "What time is it? Oh, no!"

"Oh my gosh!" Tanya said. "I told you we should have eaten closer to our gate."

"We better hurry!" Ellen said as she and her friends scrambled from their booth.

Sue put another ten-dollar bill on the table. "Please pray we make it!"

Adrian gave her a wink. "Will do. And thanks."

As they rushed from the restaurant and through the airport, rolling their carry-on cases behind them, Sue covered her heart and muttered, "Did you see the way he looked at me?"

Ellen and Tanya laughed as they tried not to leave Sue behind. Ellen felt slightly delirious.

Sue said, "If we miss our flight, that wink will have made it all worth it."

"To you, maybe," Tanya said. "Can't you walk any faster?"

"Not all of us were gifted with giraffe legs," Sue said.

Ellen, whose panic and determination had faded with her laughter, said, "There's no way we'll make it to the gate in time."

Sue slowed down. "I'm inclined to agree."

"Don't give up!" Tanya called from five feet ahead of them. "Come on, guys! *You're* the ones who wanted to go on this trip."

Ellen and Sue tried their best to keep up with Tanya, but it wasn't long before Tanya was out of sight. About ten minutes later, they saw her making her way back to them. She didn't look happy.

"We missed it?" Sue asked, when she and Ellen had caught up to their long-legged friend.

Tanya nodded.

"Don't they usually page missing passengers?" Ellen asked. "I've heard them do it many times before."

"I thought so, too," Sue said. "Do you think they called us, and we just didn't hear them?"

"I suppose that's possible," Ellen admitted. "I did think the music in the restaurant was a bit too loud."

"Now what?" Tanya asked. "The next flight to Vegas is in the morning."

"Great," Ellen muttered.

"Why do I feel like the two of you blame me for this?" Sue asked. "I didn't force you to agree to Pappadeaux."

"No one blames you," Ellen said.

Tanya shot Ellen a look. Ellen didn't need telepathic powers to know what Tanya was thinking.

"Well, you should be *thanking* me," Sue said. "I'm the one who convinced you to pack your necessities into a carry-on, in case this very thing ever happened."

"That's true," Ellen said. "So, thank you."

"But where do we go from here?" Tanya asked.

"Can't you call Brian to help us?" Sue asked Ellen.

"What?" Ellen was taken aback. "I can't expect him and his private jet to be at my beck and call."

"Why not?" Tanya asked. "I'm sure he wouldn't mind. It could save us *hours*. And maybe he'd enjoy coming to Vegas with us for a couple of days before flying back."

Ellen sighed. She'd been wanting to put a little more distance between herself and Brian, while she worked through some of her feelings, and didn't think asking him to fly them to Vegas would help her to achieve that end. Plus, he'd already arranged for them to take a very special VIP tour of Hoover Dam and was working on getting them a meeting with the mayor, who happened to be his cousin. She didn't want to overstep—she'd already overstepped.

"We could always look into hiring our own private jet," Ellen suggested.

They found a place to sit while they searched for options on their phones.

Most of the private jet services required an annual subscription, which Ellen didn't want to do for a single, one-way trip.

"Why don't we look into buying a one-way ticket to Vegas on another airline?" Ellen suggested.

"I'm already searching for one," Sue said.

Ellen and Tanya did the same, but they found all the other flights were booked.

"We could hang out at the gate where they're boarding the next flight and see if there are any last-minute cancellations," Ellen said.

"What are the odds that there will be *three*?" Sue pointed out.

"Let's just grab a hotel and come back in the morning," Tanya said.

"But what about our VIP tour of the dam?" Sue objected. "We have to be there tomorrow morning at ten. Can Brian reschedule that for us?"

In the end, Ellen broke down and called Brian.

CHAPTER TWO

A Rocky Flight

Two hours later, Ellen, Sue, and Tanya met Brian's jet on the strip of a private airport five miles away from the DFW in the windy heat. Although Brian wasn't on the plane, he'd sent Kirk to make sure Ellen and her friends were safely delivered to Vegas.

Kirk stood at the bottom of the mobile steel steps leading up to the plane entrance. He looked handsome in his khaki pants and turquoise-colored polo.

"Hello, Kirk," Tanya said. "It's nice to see you again."

Kirk took her carry-on case and stowed it in a compartment at the bottom of the jet. "It's good to see you, too, ma'am."

Tanya ascended the steps.

"Hi, there, Kirk," Sue said next. "Did you miss me? We had some good times waiting in line at Voodoo Doughnut together."

"Indeed," Kirk replied, taking her case and adding it to the compartment with Tanya's, as Sue made her way up the steps.

Ellen wondered how he *really* felt about Sue. "Hi, Kirk."

"Hello, ma'am. Mr. McManius asked me to tell you how sorry he is that he couldn't join you."

"Thank you." She handed over her carry-on.

Ellen followed Sue, who took her time going up the steps as she reminded Ellen that she had a hurt foot. Ellen's thoughts were elsewhere, however. She was wishing Brian had surprised her by canceling his Monday meetings. Even now, she hoped he'd be waiting for her on the plane and was disappointed to find that he wasn't. She told herself that it was for the best. She needed more time to sort through her feelings.

Two pairs of seats faced one another—one pair on either side of the aisle. Sue sat across from Tanya on one side of the plane, so Ellen took the seat across the aisle from Tanya, with her back to the cockpit and facing the empty seat that she supposed would be Kirk's.

Kirk soon appeared in the doorway asking if he could get them anything to drink before takeoff.

"Well, that depends," Sue said. "Is the plane as well-stocked as the limo?"

"Indeed, it is," Kirk said with a grin.

"Then margaritas all around," Sue said. "Am I right, ladies?"

"Sounds good to me," Tanya said.

"Me, too." Ellen said.

It had been a long, tiring day, and Ellen could use something to relax her.

Kirk went to the back of the plane and fixed their drinks just as the pilot entered the cabin from the cockpit.

"Hello, ladies," he said, offering each of them his hand. "My name's Jimmy. I'm looking forward to getting you safely to Las Vegas this evening."

Jimmy, who also wore khakis and a polo, was younger than Kirk—probably early thirties—and had a baby face with round cheeks that made him seem even younger.

"Nice to meet you," they said to him.

"I'm just waiting for clearance," the pilot said. "We should be ready for take-off within the next fifteen minutes or so."

"Sounds great," Sue said.

"Thank you for coming all this way to get us," Ellen added.

"It's my pleasure," Jimmy said. "I do want to warn you that we're heading into some nasty weather, so expect quite a bit of turbulence."

"Should we be worried?" Tanya asked.

"Not at all," Jimmy said. "It's nothing I haven't flown through before. I just didn't want you to be alarmed by the bumpy ride."

"How long will it be before we land?" Sue asked.

"Two-and-a-half to three hours," the pilot said.

Once the pilot had returned to the cockpit, Tanya said, "So, nine thirty, then. That's not too bad."

"It's a lot better than tomorrow," Sue said. Then, turning to Ellen, she added, "I hope you'll thank Brian on our behalf."

"Of course, I will."

"You'll have to think of something *extra special*," Sue said, "if you know what I mean."

When Ellen looked up to see Kirk blushing, her own face must have turned the color of beets. She thanked him for the drink and quickly averted her eyes. As soon as Kirk's back was turned, she made a face at Sue.

"Karma's a bitch," Sue teased.

Ellen realized Sue must be referring to her embarrassment back at Pappadeaux's with Adrian.

"Touché," Ellen said, lifting her glass in the air before taking a sip. "Mmm. This is good."

Kirk sat in the seat across from Ellen. "I'm glad you like it."

Sue had already finished hers by the time Kirk had strapped himself in.

"Delicious," Sue said.

"Should I get you another?"

"I better not. But thank you." Sue handed her empty glass to Kirk, who took it to the back of the plane before returning to his seat.

Kirk had just strapped himself back in again when the plane turned and began to take off. Ellen closed her eyes and tried to relax. No matter how often she did it, flying made her nervous.

Once they were settled in the air, Kirk asked if they were interested in watching a movie, but Sue and Tanya said they'd rather nap. Ellen decided to set her half-empty margarita glass in a nearby cupholder and close her eyes for a little while, too.

Ellen was startled awake when the plane dropped for what felt like several hundred feet. All three ladies screamed. Even Kirk wore a look of terror on his face.

Ellen's drink spilled across her chest, and the empty glass fell to her lap.

The plane abruptly stopped before ascending again, but now it swung from one side to the other, as if the wings were playing a game of see-saw.

"What's happening?" Sue cried.

"Jimmy warned us that it would get rough," Kirk replied.

"Has it ever been *this* rough?" Tanya asked.

Kirk didn't answer. He unbuckled his seat belt and fumbled past Ellen toward the cockpit.

Alone in the cabin, the three friends clung to their armrests, holding on for dear life. Ellen was trying not to be sick.

A flash of lightning illuminated the cabin. The ripping roar of thunder immediately followed.

"Do you think this is how we were meant to die?" Sue asked with a white face.

"I'm not sure if I believe that anything's meant to be," Ellen stammered.

"If it's your time, it's your time," Sue said. "There isn't a thing you can do about it. Don't you think, Tanya?"

Tears streamed down Tanya's cheeks. "I don't know, but I'm praying pretty hard right now—making all kinds of promises."

"Me, too," Ellen said, allowing her own tears to fall. "I can't leave my kids. It's too soon after Paul."

"Whoa!" Tanya cried when the nose of the plane dipped suddenly before lifting again.

"Geez Louise!" Ellen muttered through clenched teeth. "I wish Kirk would come back and tell us what the hell is going on."

"I promise to take fewer cruises," Sue said. "I'll donate what I would have spent on cruises to the Sisters of Mercy."

"Don't you already give a thousand dollars a year to them, for their missions of poverty?" Ellen asked her.

"Yes, but sometimes I wonder if I should be giving more. It's like that movie, *Schindler's List*. Remember? He says he could have saved more people if he'd made more sacrifices. Think how many mouths the cost of a cruise could feed."

Another sudden drop in altitude caused the three of them to shriek in unison.

"We actually sounded good together—our screams," Sue said. "Maybe we should start up a singing group, if we live through this."

Ellen laughed through her tears. "We could be a ghost healing singing sensation."

"We haven't been too extravagant with our money, have we?" Tanya asked.

"I don't know," Ellen said, clutching her belly and trying not to vomit. "But I guess flying in a private jet might count as *too extravagant*. Most people would have had to wait for the next flight."

Sue frowned. "Do you think we're being punished for it?"

Ellen's eyes widened as another streak of lightning illuminated the cabin. Then the plane shuddered with the roar of thunder.

"I'm not sure that God works like that," Ellen finally said. "But who the hell knows? I just know that, if we make it through this, I'll do my best to be a better person."

"Me, too," Tanya said.

"Me, three," Sue added.

"I'm so sorry that I fought with you today," Ellen said to them. "I love you both so much, and I've felt so fortunate to have you in my life."

"I feel the same way," Tanya said through her tears.

"Me, too," Sue said. "Even if I do tease you both too much. I hope I've never hurt your feelings."

The plane swung hard to the right and then back to the left—the wings playing see-saw again.

"I appreciate your sense of humor," Ellen said to Sue, praying she wouldn't be sick. "And I'm sorry I called you a hypochondriac."

"When did you call me a hypochondriac? I don't remember that."

"Oh, at Panera. I don't think I said it out loud."

"I'm not a hypochondriac," Sue said. "I just happen to take my health seriously."

Ellen regretted saying anything and kept her mouth shut.

Then another flash of lightning lit up the cabin, and Ellen braced herself for the trembling roar that followed.

"If we live," Sue said, "I promise to try harder to lose weight."

"Me, too," Ellen said.

"Me, three," Tanya chimed in.

"Stop," Sue said to Tanya. "You don't get to say that."

"Yes, I do," Tanya said in an angry voice. "You don't get to be the queen of losing weight, just because you're heavier. I hate it when you make me feel like my concern about my weight is trivial."

"I'm sorry," Sue said. "I'd just give anything to have your body."

"I'm sorry I snapped at you," Tanya said. "I'm so scared."

"Me, too," Sue said.

"Me, three," Ellen said.

Kirk emerged from the cockpit and scrambled to his seat, strapping himself in.

"What's happening?" Ellen asked.

"Jimmy wants to land in Phoenix," Kirk said. "This storm is too dangerous for us to remain in the air."

"Okay," Ellen said.

"Sounds good to me," Sue said.

"Is he worried about the landing?" Tanya asked.

Kirk swallowed before saying, "I don't think so. He knows what he's doing."

Ellen did not feel reassured.

"I guess we'll miss that VIP tour of Hoover Dam after all," Sue said.

"At least we'll be alive," Ellen said.

Tanya, still sobbing, said, "I hope you're right, Ellen."

"We're going to be fine, ladies," Kirk said. "Jimmy's a fine pilot." Then he added, "I'll rent a limo and drive you into Boulder City after we land. You won't miss the tour. I promise."

The plane swung dangerously far to the right. Sue moaned. Ellen gritted her teeth, fearing the plane would roll. She closed her eyes and held onto her armrests as the plane descended in jerks and sweeps.

"Maybe something powerful doesn't want us in Boulder City!" Tanya wailed. "Maybe this was a mistake!"

Ellen said nothing as she gripped the armrests and silently prayed that they would land safely. She couldn't bear to be taken away from her kids.

"Please," she begged.

Suddenly, the plane dropped toward the ground, as if the engines had stopped running. All four passengers screamed. Ellen kept her eyes closed and braced herself for the worst.

Her stomach dropped when the plane went into a nosedive.

"Oh, God!" Tanya moaned.

After what seemed like a very long time, the plane straightened out, though it continued to wobble. Ellen flinched when the wheels hit against the ground and screeched before bouncing back into the air. Sue shrieked as the wheels hit a second time.

Ellen glanced out the window. Where were the lights? What kind of airport didn't have lights?

The sudden force of the plane braking threw Ellen and Tanya forward, only their safety harnesses holding them in their seats. Ellen reached across the aisle to hold Tanya's hand. Tanya took it and then reached out for Sue's. Ellen closed her eyes as the plane bounced her like a basketball, rattling her teeth.

When the plane finally came to a screeching halt, Ellen opened her eyes and looked around. Sue and Tanya wore looks of surprise and glee on their faces.

"We made it!" Ellen cried to Kirk, who was unstrapping his safety belt.

"Is everybody okay?" Kirk asked Ellen and her friends.

Tanya was sobbing so hard that she couldn't speak, but she nodded and managed a smile.

"Thank God, we made it," Sue said. "Only, now, I'll have to keep all of my promises."

Jimmy emerged from the cockpit. "Everyone all right?"

"That depends on your definition of *all right*," Sue said. "We're alive, anyway."

"Thanks to you," Ellen added.

"Were you ever worried we weren't going to make it?" Tanya asked the pilot.

Jimmy busted out laughing. "You bet I was. It's a miracle we made it, if you ask me."

That didn't reassure Ellen at all.

"Where are we?" Ellen asked. "I doubt that darkness out there is an airport."

"Salt River Reservation," Jimmy said. "The storm blew us east of Scottsdale. It was the best I could do under the circumstances."

"I'm not complaining," Ellen said, glancing at her phone for the time, which was 9:15 p.m.

"An emergency vehicle is on the way," Jimmy assured them. "The medics will transport us to the nearest hospital, to make sure we're all right."

"We don't have time for that," Sue insisted. "We need to get to Boulder City."

Kirk took out his phone. "I'll order a limo from Scottsdale."

While Kirk arranged for a vehicle, Jimmy opened the cabin door to the outside, where the rain pelted the desert in darkness. Barely visible through the deluge were the lights of a nearby city.

"Would you ladies care for another margarita while we wait?" Kirk asked after he ended his call.

"Heck yeah," Sue said. "That's exactly what we need."

Ellen busted out laughing as she made her way back to her seat. If they were going to be stranded, at least it was in style.

Halfway into her margarita, her phone vibrated in her lap. It was Brian calling.

"Hi, there," she said.

"My God, Ellen. I just got off the phone with Jimmy. Are you all right?"

"I'm fine. We're all fine."

"I can't believe this happened. I wish I would have been there . . . with you."

Ellen's stomach fluttered, and a tingle of pleasure trickled down her spine. But then, as usual, a wave of guilt clenched her stomach as she considered how her feelings would affect Paul, if he were watching her. They'd spent over thirty years together. Didn't he deserve more from her?

"Did Jimmy say whether the plane had suffered any damage?" she asked.

"That doesn't matter. I don't care about that. I care about you."

"Well, like I said, I'm fine. You needn't worry, Brian."

"Needn't worry? You could have been killed."

"But I wasn't."

"Thank God."

"And don't forget to thank Jimmy. I'm sure he had something to do with it, too."

Brian chuckled. "Maybe a little. I've already promised him a raise for keeping my girl alive."

Ellen laughed. "I think Kirk deserves one, too."

"I want to see you," Brian said suddenly. "To make sure you're all right."

"I told you, I'm fine."

"I won't stay long."

"When?"

"I'm not sure yet. How long will you be in Boulder City?"

"We packed for two weeks, but we don't really know."

"I'll come as soon as I can. I hope you get some rest."

"Thanks, Brian. Sweet dreams."

"Always," he said in a husky voice.

After she'd ended the call, Sue asked, "When's he coming?"

"He's not sure."

"I had a feeling he would," Tanya said.

The last thing Ellen wanted was for Kirk to overhear details about her love life with his boss, so she shushed her friends when his back was turned.

As she sat there in the plane, sipping on her margarita, she said a little prayer to Paul. She wanted him to know that she hadn't forgotten him, that she still loved him very much, and that their lives together had been the best part of her life. Tears welled in her eyes as she promised him that he could never be replaced or forgotten.

"You okay?" Tanya asked her.

Ellen nodded. "Just emotional."

With a fresh margarita in hand, Sue lifted her glass. "If there was ever a time to be emotional, I would say surviving an emergency crash landing qualifies."

"Amen," Tanya said as she clinked her glass to Sue's.

"Amen," Ellen echoed, clinking her glass against those of her friends.

CHAPTER THREE

Boulder Dam Hotel

It was nearly two in the morning when Kirk woke Ellen and her friends, who had slept in the limo during the four-hour drive from the Salt River Reservation to Boulder City. Despite the comfortable leather seats, Ellen awoke with a stiff neck.

The exterior lighting of the Boulder Dam Hotel illuminated a Colonial Revival with a wide pillared porch, white painted brick, and two stories of windows—most of which were dark. Even the lobby appeared dark from the street.

"Thank goodness it isn't storming outside," Tanya said as she yawned.

Kirk handed them their carryon luggage from the trunk with promises to have their other bags delivered from the airport in Vegas as soon as possible. He left them at the front of their hotel and headed to his own, the Quality Inn on the other side of town.

"Poor guy," Ellen said as they walked up the sidewalk to the entrance. "At least we got to sleep. He must be exhausted."

They stepped onto a wide porch, where wall sconces softly illuminated a few tables and chairs.

The quaint lobby was cold and quiet, and, except for a small light over a wooden stairwell and a dim lamp on the front desk, dark. Beneath the lamp was an envelope with Sue's name written on it.

"Those must be our keys," Ellen said quietly.

As she reached for them, the lamp flickered, startling her. A chill sent goosebumps up and down her arms.

"I didn't mean to frighten you, dear," the voice of a young woman came from the darkness behind the front desk.

It made all three women jump.

"We didn't see you there," Ellen said.

She still couldn't see the young woman.

"We've been expecting you," she said, without coming into the light. "I hope you find what you're looking for."

"Thank you. We do, too," Sue said.

"I should have known you'd be night people," the young woman said. "I'm a night person, too. My father never liked it, when I was a girl. But I have found night people to be much more courteous than morning people. Wouldn't you agree? Night people tiptoe in the dark and gently close doors, so as not to disturb the morning people while they're sleeping. But morning people don't show the same courtesy. They slam doors, bang pots and pans, and talk loudly, as if they believe all people should be awake early, too."

"You might be right about that," Sue said softly with a chuckle. "Let's ask Tanya. She's a morning person."

"We're not *all* discourteous," Tanya said with a smile.

The woman said nothing in reply.

Ellen handed each of them their keys. "We're on the second floor."

"Oh, which way to the elevator?" Sue asked the woman behind the desk.

The lamp turned out, and, if the woman said anything, they didn't hear her.

"I think it's this way," Ellen said, reaching for her phone, to use as a light. "Oh, darn. My phone died."

"Mine did, too," Tanya whispered. "That's not suspicious."

Sue illuminated the lobby with her flashlight app. "Portable charger. Come on."

In the circle of Sue's flashlight app, the lobby appeared cozy, with a grouping of furniture around a fireplace. A sign for the elevator was to the left of the mantel.

They followed Sue into the elevator and rode to the second floor, where they said goodnight before retreating to their individual rooms.

Ellen walked into an art deco suite with a photo of Boris Karloff, a 1930's horror movie and television star, who, according to a sign near the photo, had slept in this very room.

Remembering the actor for his role as Frankenstein's monster, Ellen giggled as she readied for bed.

Once in her pajamas, she was brushing her teeth over the bathroom sink, when she thought she saw someone in the mirror, someone standing behind her. She gasped and turned but found no one there. She took a few slow breaths to calm herself and decided she was just tired and traumatized. She rinsed and turned out the bathroom light before climbing into bed.

While she set her alarm on her phone, which was charging on the nightstand beside her beneath a bright lamp, Ellen thought she saw someone in her peripheral vision. Again, when she looked across the room toward the bathroom, there was no one there.

Was someone trying to make contact with her?

In both cases, she hadn't been able to tell if it was a man or a woman. It had been a transparent figure without distinct features.

She climbed out of bed and took her portable EMF detector from her purse. When she turned it on, she wasn't surprised to find a higher-than-normal reading.

"Is someone here?" she asked softly, trembling a little. No matter how many times she'd interacted with ghosts, there was always an element of fear. One never knew when one was dealing with a benevolent or malevolent being. "Is there something you wish to say to me?"

She stood in the silence for many minutes and, when nothing happened, she climbed back into bed, thinking she must be imagining things. She lay the EMF detector beside her phone on the nightstand, turned off the lamp, and tried to go to sleep. She needed to be up in five hours to meet Sue and Tanya for breakfast before heading to the Hoover Dam for their VIP tour.

As she was about to fall asleep, Ellen sensed something—cold air on her cheek. She opened her eyes and froze. In the darkness, a man's face bent close to hers, his eyes narrowed, his dark brows furrowed.

"Don't stir up trouble," he said just before he vanished.

Ellen sat up and turned on the lamp, scanning the room for signs of an intruder. Trembling and gasping, she checked beneath the bed and in the bathtub to be sure there was no one there—no living, breathing person. She needed to rule out every possibility before accepting the notion that she'd just been visited by a ghost.

Unsure if she should awaken her friends or wait until breakfast to tell them what had happened, Ellen stood over her phone, wringing her hands for several minutes before deciding to let her friends get their sleep. Was it possible that she had dreamt it? She'd been on the verge of sleep. Maybe she'd only imagined it.

Just to be safe, she took a saltshaker from her purse and created a circle of protection around her bed. She added a cup of water to each of the cardinal points—which she found using her phone—to be extra cautious. Then she closed the circle with the now-familiar incantation:

Guardians of the North, South, East, and West,
Elements of Earth, Air, Fire, and Water,
Bless this circle and protect those within,
Whether father, mother, son, or daughter.
No unwanted entities shall enter,
And safety shall prevail in the center.
This circle is cast.
Grant it shall last.

She climbed back beneath the covers and, leaving the lamp on, tried to go back to sleep; but she opened her eyes every few minutes, checking. What if she *hadn't* imagined him? And what if he returned?

In the morning, as Ellen dressed for the day in loose black pants and a peach floral summer top, she decided to keep what had happened during the night to herself. She'd probably imagined it, being nearly asleep, and, even if she hadn't, a warning from a ghost would only frighten Tanya into wanting to leave.

Tired from her restless night, she went downstairs to the lobby, where she was supposed to meet her friends, and finding herself to be the first one there, walked around admiring the art on the walls as she waited. Two men sat on the sofa, across from the empty fireplace, talking.

"Good morning," the woman behind the front desk said to Ellen.

Obviously not the one who had greeted them the night before, she looked to be in her late forties and had curly red hair that fell to her shoulders.

"Good morning," Ellen replied.

"If you want a cooked-to-order breakfast, you better get on the wait list. There's about a fifteen-minute wait this morning."

Ellen approached the desk. "Yes, thank you. There are three of us."

"Oh, are you Sue Graham?"

"No, I'm Ellen Mohr. But Sue's in my party."

"Oh, good. I just wanted to apologize for not having anyone there to check you in last night. With this flu going around, I've been short on staff. And you'd think people would avoid this place, like the plague, but we've been inundated with reporters and paranormal investigators, like you."

Ellen furrowed her brows. "But there *was* someone here last night—a younger woman."

Sue and Tanya caught up to her at the front desk just as the redhead behind it frowned. "I have no idea who that could have been. What did she look like?"

"Who?" Sue asked.

"The woman from last night," Ellen explained.

"Well, it was dark," Sue said.

"We didn't get a good look at her," Ellen added.

"Hmm," the redhead said. "The important thing is that you ladies found your keys and your rooms without any problem. Did you sleep okay?"

Ellen glanced at Sue and Tanya.

"We had a rough flight," Sue finally said. "It was hard to sleep after that."

Tanya nodded. "The room was fine. It wasn't the room."

"I'm sorry to hear you didn't sleep well," the woman behind the counter said. "I hope you get better rest tonight."

"Thank you," Ellen said.

The woman lifted her walkie talkie and said, "Copy that." Then she turned to Ellen and her friends. "Martha says your table is ready."

They had just been seated at the only vacant table in the restaurant when a young woman approached with a notepad and pen. Instead of asking for their order, she said, "Are you the three ladies of Ghost Healers, Inc.?"

"Um," Ellen glanced at Sue and Tanya.

"Have you begun your paranormal investigation into the causes of the Phantom Flu and the ghost sightings in Boulder City?" the young woman asked.

"We just arrived," Sue said. "And the only thing on my mind right now is the Big Dam Breakfast."

"I thought we were going to count calories," Tanya murmured.

"Not while we're traveling," Sue said. "It's hard enough to keep track at home."

"Do you have any theories yet about what might be causing the flu-like symptoms?" the woman asked.

"Not yet," Ellen said.

"I'll update my blog as soon as we know anything," Sue added. "Now, if you don't mind, we'd like to order breakfast."

"One more question, please?"

The three friends sighed.

"Can I shadow you as you conduct your investigation?"

All three shook their heads.

"I'm sorry," Ellen said. "We can't work like that. I hope you understand."

The redhead from the front desk approached the table and asked to have a private word with the young woman.

"Talk about rude," Sue complained as she opened her menu.

"She's just trying to do her job," Tanya said.

"I used to fantasize about being a celebrity," Sue said as she glanced over her menu. "But now I understand the desire to keep out of the limelight."

Ellen and Tanya looked at each other and giggled.

"We're hardly celebrities," Tanya said.

"Speak for yourself," Sue said with a smile.

Ellen leaned forward. "Do y'all think the young woman from last night…do you think she was a ghost?"

"Let's not jump to conclusions," Sue said.

Just a few years ago, if someone would have asked Ellen to bet money on who, out of her or Sue, would say those last two lines, she would have bet the other way and would have lost.

After a delicious breakfast, the three friends decided to visit the hotel's museum, since they had time to kill before they needed to leave for the VIP tour of the dam. They returned upstairs and passed a gift shop and a couple of art galleries before they arrived at what turned out to be a top-notch museum showcasing the construction of the Hoover Dam. A mural with life-size illustrations of some of the key people—including Roosevelt and Hoover—greeted them on one wall. The exhibits were interactive and interesting. Ellen had already known some of the history—the part about the dam being built during the Great Depression as a way for public works to provide jobs for Americans at a time when jobs were hard to find. She also knew that the dam was considered one of the great engineering wonders of the world, having tamed the Colorado River—known as the Red Bull, because of the red silt that gave it its color—so that the southwest could become something more than a desert.

But she hadn't been familiar with some of the other details. She hadn't known that housing hadn't been established for the workers before they arrived and that they'd had to live in tents and makeshift shacks until housing could be built for them. She also hadn't given much thought to the intolerably hot climate the three thousand workers had labored in, or the snakes and other critters that often crossed their paths. And they had no air conditioning to go home to.

"There was nothing out here," Tanya muttered as they read through the exhibits. "No food or water, no stores, no hospital. Everything had to be built while they were already working on the dam. How did they manage in those first months without a hospital?"

Sue pointed to another display. "Sounds like they made a race out of building these tunnels. Six Companies would have to pay $3000 for every day they went over their deadline. The crews were encouraged to compete against one other, to see who could make the most progress each day."

"That's scary," Tanya said, "considering they were working with dynamite."

They approached an exhibit with four panels, each with a handle, and above them was a poster asking, "What's my job?" The first read *Nipper*, and when Ellen lifted the panel, beneath it was an explanation: A nipper kept the miner supplied with dynamite and steel, for drilling. The next panel read *Juicer*. Ellen lifted it to read: the one who sets off the blast after everyone else has moved to safety. The third panel read *Scaler*.

Sue lifted the panel and said, "Oh, I remember reading about the high-scalers. They hung from ropes and scaled the face of the dam for loose rock, knocking it down below. I remember reading that occasional miscommunication between the crews resulted in the muckers below getting injured from the falling rock."

"So, the muckers were the ones who cleared the fallen rock at the bottom?" Ellen asked, lifting the panel to see if Sue had used the word correctly. "Yep. They cleared mud and rock away after the blast."

"That doesn't sound very fun, does it," Sue said without inflection.

"No, it does not," Tanya agreed.

They moved to a giant wall depicting the scale of the canyon. Ellen hadn't realized that the canyon where the dam was built was called Black Canyon—not Boulder Canyon. According to the exhibit, the project had been called the Boulder Dam Project before the official site had been chosen, and the name stuck even after it had been determined that Black Canyon was the best location for the dam.

The display of the canyon included a model with cables that visitors could manipulate back and forth. Ellen was struck by the sheer size of it—by the danger the height presented to the workers who sometimes fell to their deaths.

"Well, this is good to know," Sue said, pointing to a nearby sign. "Despite rumors to the contrary, no one was buried alive beneath the concrete."

"That *is* good to know," Ellen agreed. "But ninety-six men *did* die during its construction, even if they aren't buried beneath it. I wonder if some of those victims are the ghosts people claim to have seen, people who have commented on your blog."

"Yes, but like you said," Tanya began, "why now?"

The museum ended with a small theater with a ten-minute film showing footage that was taken during the dam's construction. They didn't stay for it all, because it was soon time to leave for their tour.

As they walked past the front desk, the woman with the red hair said, "I hope you have a dam good time!"

Outside in the heat, Ellen turned to her friends. "She was rather enthusiastic, wasn't she?"

"At least she wasn't a ghost," Tanya said.

"True," Ellen agreed.

"Not that we know of, anyway," Sue said. "According to reports, just about anyone around here *could* be one, so stay alert."

CHAPTER FOUR

A Dam Good Tour

Kirk met Ellen, Sue, and Tanya with the limo outside of the Boulder Dam Hotel at 9:30 a.m., as planned, and dropped them off at the Hoover Dam on his way to Vegas, to retrieve their luggage. Although he looked better than he had when he'd dropped them at the hotel in the middle of the night, Ellen thought he could still use a full night's sleep.

Not many tourists were walking along the top of the dam as Ellen, Sue, and Tanya made their way to their designated meeting place—a flagpole flanked by two winged statues.

As they approached the statues, Sue reached out and touched one. "I overheard someone say you're supposed to rub the toes of the statue for luck. We may as well."

"Think of all the germs," Tanya said. "If you want to catch the Phantom Flu, then rub away."

"I hadn't thought of that," Sue said, staring at her hand as if it were an alien. "Anyone got any hand sanitizer?"

Tanya pulled a small bottle from her purse and gave it to Sue.

"It's not contagious, remember?" Ellen pointed out.

"That's what they're saying," Sue said. "But you never know."

They walked around the beautiful sculptures and read the nearby memorial, dedicated to the men who died "to make the desert bloom." It was a low relief panel depicting a man emerging from the water in front of the dam. Around him were lightning bolts shooting from a thunder cloud and grains, fruits, and vegetables shooting from the earth.

"Ellen!"

Ellen turned to find Brian waving at her as he headed toward her from the other side of the dam. He looked handsome in his loose-fitting jeans and a short-sleeved blue shirt that brought out the silver in his hair and the gray in his eyes.

"What are you doing here?" Ellen said, laughing with surprise as she and Brian met up.

Beside him was another man, probably in his early thirties. Ellen supposed he must be the tour guide.

Brian took her in his arms and pecked her cheek. "Surprise."

"It *is* a surprise," she said. "You must have hopped on the first flight out this morning."

"I did. I wasn't sure I'd make it here in time."

Ellen noticed the others hovering around them awkwardly.

Brian stepped back to give Sue and Tanya hugs and then said, "This is Matt. He's my cousin's son."

"Nice to meet you," they said.

"Look at that," Sue said with a smile. "We made a dam friend."

Ellen shook her head. Tanya rolled her eyes.

"He's worked here as an engineer for over ten years and knows everything there is to know about the Hoover Dam."

"I wouldn't go that far," Matt said with a grin.

"We appreciate you doing this for us," Ellen said to Matt.

"Yes, thank you," Tanya and Sue added.

"Are we ready to get started?" Brian asked.

"We're *dam* ready," Sue said.

Ellen hoped Sue didn't plan on making the same joke throughout the whole dam tour.

They followed Matt across the dam to the Arizona elevator tower, which was a work of art. Shiny golden elevator doors made of brass were situated beneath five concrete bas-reliefs depicting Native American symbols. Matt entered a code into a panel.

"You weren't kidding when you said we'd get the VIP tour," Ellen murmured as they entered the art deco elevators.

Brian beamed down at her. "Very few visitors get to see what we're going to see."

"This sort of feels like Willy Wonka's chocolate factory," Sue said.

Matt chuckled. "Not quite. We're heading down to the cooling unit inspection tunnel, inside the concrete base of the dam."

The elevator gave a little jolt before descending, which caused the three friends to gasp and then laugh. Ellen supposed they would be on edge for a while after their crash landing. She clutched her jaw as her ears popped just before the elevator doors opened.

They followed Matt into a dark concrete corridor where it forked into two long tunnels that seemed to go on forever.

"The water is held back by the weight of the dam," Matt said. "It's made of 3.25 million cubic yards of concrete."

"That's dam impressive," Sue said.

"And even more impressive is the volume of water it's capable of holding in Lake Mead," Matt said. "Maximum capacity is 9.3 trillion gallons."

"Geez Louise," Ellen said.

"Back in the days before the dam," Matt said, "the Colorado River would flood in the spring and destroy everything in its wake. At other times, it would all but dry up. Controlling the Colorado was necessary for the development of the southwest."

He led them down one of the tunnels. Brian and Tanya had to stoop over so as not to hit their heads. Matt stepped over a steel grate covering what appeared to be a bottomless pit, and Ellen and Brian followed.

Tanya paused before the grate. "How far down does that hole go?"

"About four hundred feet," Matt said.

Ellen offered her hand to Tanya. "Come on, girlfriend. You got this."

Tanya stepped over the grate, but now Sue hesitated.

"How much weight can that grate take?" Sue asked. Then she added, "That sounded like something from Dr. Seuss."

Matt chuckled. "I expect it can hold about half a ton or so."

"I just want to make sure there's no chance that I might break it," Sue said. "Because digging my body out of that abyss would be no easy task."

"We'd probably leave you there," Tanya teased.

"Oh, no you wouldn't, because then I'd haunt you for the rest of your life."

"Come on, Sue, and stop stalling," Ellen complained.

As Ellen took her hand, Sue cautiously put one foot on the grate and then half-hopped over.

Matt led them to a vent in the face of the dam, from where they could see the power plant and the bypass bridge.

"I read that the dam is over seven hundred feet high," Sue said.

"Seven hundred and twenty-six, to be exact," Matt said.

"Imagine what it must have been like for the workers who fell to their deaths," Sue murmured.

"No, thank you," Tanya murmured back.

"Didn't I read that ninety-six men were killed on the job?" Ellen asked.

"That's right," Matt said.

"It's a wonder there weren't more," Brian said.

"That number only includes those who died while working on the dam," Matt explained. "It doesn't include anyone who died of heat-stroke or other illnesses away from the dam site."

Matt then took them down to the Arizona visitors' gallery, where he said *Transformers* and *Chevy Chase's Vegas Vacation* had been filmed. The gallery was vacant of people.

"Why aren't there visitors here today?" Ellen asked, wondering if the recent paranormal activity had kept people away.

"The Reclamation Bureau doesn't offer tours on this side anymore."

As they followed him down the gallery, Sue asked, "Why not?"

"The Nevada side is a mirror image of the Arizona side," Matt said. "So, you see basically the same thing here as you do there."

"But that still doesn't explain why they don't do them on this side," Tanya pointed out.

Matt led them into an open area that looked down over the power plant. "The Reclamation Bureau decided to restrict this side for safety reasons."

"Why?" Ellen asked.

"Well," Matt's face turned pink. "Supposedly, it's haunted."

Ellen and her friends exchanged glances, but, when Matt grinned, they laughed.

"Good one," Brian said to Matt.

"A *dam* good one," Sue giggled.

"They do say this side is haunted," Matt said, "but that's not why they restricted it. It's really more to do with safety, in case evacuation is necessary."

"But we're safe?" Tanya asked.

"*Dam* safe," Matt said leading them to a gallery of infographics, where he then explained how the intake towers sucked in water and sent it through the powerplant to the turbines, where electricity was made.

"This power plant provides about four billion kilowatts of electricity per year to over a million people in Nevada, Arizona, and California."

"Wow," Brian said.

Tanya gripped the rail and looked down at the plant. "This place is massive."

Sue chuckled. "*Dam* massive."

After donning hard hats, they followed Matt into the Arizona powerhouse, where the mechanics and maintenance crews worked on parts of the generating units.

From there, Matt led them to the contractors' adit, where the builders of the dam could access what was once a divergence tunnel. He showed them the holes where the dam builders once placed dynamite to blast through the mountain to create the tunnels. Ellen and the others felt the holes for themselves, just before a low roar sounded through the rock.

"What in the world?" Tanya muttered.

"That's just water moving through the penstock," Matt explained.

"What's a penstock?" Ellen asked.

"A large pipe—in this case, a pipe with a thirty-foot diameter."

"Creepy," Brian said. "I can feel the water vibrating the wall."

"Wait a minute," Sue said, stopping. "Is that a leak?"

Tanya's face turned white. "Is the dam leaking?"

Ellen's eyes widened with surprise at the trickle of water on the rough, rocky wall of the tunnel.

"Not a dam leak," Matt said. "A natural hot spring from an extinct volcano."

"Seriously?" Brian said. "That's cool."

"You mean *hot*," Sue teased.

"Oh, Sue," Ellen said, shaking her head.

At the end of the tunnel, Mike showed them a reinforced steel flood door. "In case we get a leak, this door will keep the power plant dry."

"So, the dam does leak sometimes," Tanya said.

"Not the dam," Mike said. "The pipes that take the water from the intake towers to the turbines might occasionally leak."

He then led them into what was once a visitor's gallery with a big window overlooking one of the penstocks. The pipe was encased in concrete and was situated in a tunnel of rock.

He pointed through the window. "That was one of the original divergence tunnels. The Colorado River was diverted through that tunnel while the workers constructed the dam."

Ellen felt a chill in the room.

"Is this the area that's believed to be haunted?" Sue asked.

Matt shrugged. "I'm not sure."

Tanya arched a brow. "Why do you ask? Do you sense something?"

"Maybe," Sue said.

"Matt, would you mind if we took a moment to try and make contact?" Ellen asked.

"Make contact?" he repeated.

Brian told Matt about Ellen and her friends' experience with paranormal investigations.

"Oh, sure," Matt finally said.

Ellen pulled her pendulum from her purse, along with her EMF detector. Although the reading was within the normal range, it was on the higher end.

Tanya took a shaker of salt from her purse. "I don't want to take any chances," she said to Ellen. Then to Matt, she asked, "Do you mind? It doesn't take much."

Before Matt could answer, Tanya began sprinkling a circle of salt around them on the tiled floor of the visitors' gallery, saying, "Don't break this circle."

Sue turned to Matt. "If I flick my Bic, will I cause an explosion?"

"No, ma'am. But there's no smoking in here."

"Good to know," Sue said.

Once the circle was complete, Sue flicked her lighter to produce a flame. Ellen held her pendulum from the end of the string and waited until it was very still.

Then Ellen said, "Spirits of the other realm. We come in peace and with good intentions. If anyone is here with us today, we'd like to communicate with you with this pendulum. Come toward the light and feed from it. If you're here, please make the pendulum swing."

Ellen glanced up at Brian, who was watching her expectantly. Matt wore a frown. She could tell he was a skeptic.

"Spirits of the other realm," Sue said. "Please let us know if you're here. We want to help you to be heard. Move the pendulum as a sign to us of your presence."

Ellen gasped when the pendulum began to swing toward and away from her.

"Are you moving that?" Matt whispered to Ellen.

Brian lifted his hand toward Matt, to silence him as Ellen whispered to Sue, "It responded to you. Keep going."

Sue nodded. "Spirit of the other realm, thank you for your sign. We appreciate that. Do you have a message for us? If so, please move the pendulum in the opposite direction."

The string began turning in a circle before it swung to Ellen's right and left.

"Give me your pennies," Tanya said to Ellen.

"What?" Ellen asked. "Why?"

"Got any change?" Tanya asked the men.

They emptied their pockets. Ellen gave Tanya her coin purse, which was filled with pennies she'd been meaning to get rid of. Tanya poured the coins on the tiled floor just outside of their circle of salt.

"Ask the spirit to use the coins to spell out a message," Tanya told Sue.

Ellen was impressed by Tanya's quick thinking, but before Sue could ask the question, the big window overlooking the penstock cracked. The humidity from the old divergence tunnel caused the window to fog up, and before anyone could react, letters appeared in the condensation that spelled: *Help!*

"What the hell?" Matt exclaimed.

"Help," Brian read aloud.

Ellen noticed the pennies near her feet, which had been rearranged into the shapes of six letters: *BEWARE.*

"I'm afraid to leave the circle," Tanya whispered.

"I need to report this window as soon as possible, ladies," Matt said. "It may have been caused by a sudden change in pressure, which could be a problem."

"How do you explain the writing?" Sue challenged.

"That must have been there already," Matt said. "It only became visible with the condensation."

"And the pennies?" Tanya asked.

Matt looked down for the first time. "Did one of you do that?"

They all shook their heads.

But the dam worker didn't appear to believe them.

CHAPTER FIVE

Interviews

Once Matt had gone to alert the other engineers of the broken window overlooking the penstock in the old Arizona viewing room, Ellen, Sue, and Tanya took the tour everyone else took on the Nevada side. Meanwhile, Brian went to meet Jimmy at the hangar the plane had been towed to for repairs.

After the tour, the three friends sat at a table on the patio of the High Scale Café enjoying their lunch when Ellen decided to tell them about the ghost she may or may not have seen in her room during the previous night.

"Why didn't you tell us before?" Tanya asked.

"I wasn't sure if I'd imagined it. I was so tired."

"If that's true," Sue said with a frown, "then why are you telling us now? What changed your mind?"

Ellen stared at the larger-than-life statue of a high scaler situated near the front of the café. The figure was forever rappelling along the faux canyon wall.

"I suppose I'm confused," she finally said. "The woman in the lobby last night—do we agree she was likely a ghost?"

"Maybe," Sue said.

"Probably," Tanya said.

"Didn't she seem to be glad about our arrival?" Ellen asked.

"I suppose so," Sue said. "She'd even commented that she was expecting us, which is what made me believe she was the concierge."

"And the ghost in the dam," Ellen said. "It asked for our help and told us to beware."

"So?" Tanya asked. "What are you getting at?"

"Well, why would the ghost in my room—if it wasn't a dream or my imagination—tell me not to stir up trouble?"

"Yeah, I see what you're saying," Tanya said. "We're getting different messages from different ghosts—some want us here and at least one doesn't."

"Maybe our interview with Mary Jane McGinty and her daughter will shed some light on what's going on in this city," Sue said optimistically.

Thirty minutes later, Ellen and her friends took a cab to the McGinty residence—a one-story cottage with a wooden front porch and gray siding. In lieu of grass, the yard was landscaped with pea gravel divided in half by a flagstone sidewalk leading up to the house from the street.

Mary Jane McGinty, a petite woman in her forties with short brown hair, greeted them at the door and invited them inside. They walked directly into the living room. It looked tidy with its laminate wood flooring and blue shaggy area rug flanked by two couches and a recliner arranged around a coffee table. Mary Jane invited them to take a seat on one of the couches and asked if they wanted anything to drink. They declined, trying not to speak too loudly, because a young woman with long frazzled brown hair was sleeping in the recliner. Mary Jane explained that that was her daughter, Erin, who had come down with the Phantom Flu in mid-April, not long after she'd first been visited by the ghost.

"It goes wherever she goes," Mary Jane said of the ghost. "Even before she got sick, when she stayed the night with friends, he visited her there."

"We don't know that for sure, Mom," Erin said without opening her eyes.

"Why do you say that?" Sue asked.

Erin opened her eyes and coughed several times. "Because I didn't see him that night, at the sleep over. My friend's mom did."

"What did your friend's mom see?" Ellen asked.

"She said she saw a man. She could see right through him. And, he was stroking my hair."

Ellen shuddered. That sounded creepy—being stroked by a ghost.

"My friend's mom said the ghost seemed fatherly," Erin added. "She didn't think he would hurt me, but…"

"You don't agree?" Tanya asked.

Erin shook her head as she coughed again. "I've told him to stay away from me, and he won't. Maybe my friend's mom made up that story to make me feel better."

"Has he ever threatened you?" Ellen asked.

"He's never said a word. He just looms over me. Isn't that threatening enough?"

"He might be coming to you for help," Sue said. "Has anyone in your family recently passed?"

"My husband died ten years ago," Mrs. McGinty said. "We haven't lost anyone else."

"It doesn't look like Dad," Erin quickly said. "I can't see his face clearly, but this man is taller and skinnier. Besides, Dad wouldn't do this to me."

"Tell us a little about your husband," Ellen said to Mary Jane, while Erin finished another bout of coughing. "Where did you meet?"

Mary Jane smiled. "Las Vegas. He grew up here in Boulder City, and I was vacationing with my family."

"What did he do for a living?" Sue asked.

"He worked for the dam," she said.

"Oh?" Ellen asked. "In what capacity?"

"Maintenance crew. Do you really think this ghost that's been bothering Erin is my late husband?"

Ellen lifted her palms. "We don't know, which is why we'd like to investigate, tonight, if you don't mind."

"Why not *now*?" Erin asked.

"For our cameras to collect good data, we need as little light as possible," Sue explained. "Ghosts feed on energy, like electricity, and they sometimes appear to us as light. That's why they're harder to see during the daytime."

"Our cameras are also very sensitive to light," Ellen added. "We don't want to mistake a glare or a reflection for an apparition."

"Oh," Erin said.

"So, could we come back tonight, around eight o'clock?" Sue asked.

"Of course," Mary Jane McGinty said. "We're grateful for anything you can do. Another paranormal investigation team came last month and did one of those sage ceremonies that's supposed to rid a place of spirits, but the ghost came back the next day."

"Did the other investigators share any findings with you?" Tanya asked.

Erin shook her head. "They didn't find *anything*. I could see the ghost the whole time they were here with their cameras and instruments, but no one else could. The ghost appeared to be speaking, but I couldn't hear him—nobody could. And they acted like it was all in my head."

"I highly doubt that, considering the other strange things that have been going on in Boulder City," Sue said, "but we have to ask. Are you taking any medication?"

"An antidepressant," Mary Jane said. "But she didn't start taking it until after she saw the ghost, after she became sleep deprived."

Ellen sighed. "You poor thing. I'm so sorry this has been happening to you. And I promise we'll do everything we can to help."

"Before we go," Tanya began, "can you tell us a little more about the encounters? Are you usually asleep, or about to fall asleep, when he appears?"

"Not always," Erin said. "I saw him once in the kitchen. I was looking in the fridge for something to eat, and I had a feeling that someone else was in the room. I thought it was my mom, but when I turned to look, no one was there. That's when I realized it was him."

"You didn't see him?" Sue asked.

"Not at first, but I didn't need to. I knew he was there. I could feel him. Have you ever felt that before? That feeling that someone's there, even when you can't see them?"

Ellen nodded. They all had. "So, then what happened?"

"I went down the hall to my room, and when I turned back to tell him not to follow me, I caught a glance of him just before he disappeared. I said, 'Please, leave me alone,' like I always do. He left but came back just as I was going to sleep."

"And what did he do when he came back?" Sue asked.

"Just loomed over me, as usual. So, I got up and came in here."

"She goes back and forth throughout the night," Mary Jane added.

"I usually can't sleep until daytime. He doesn't bother me during the day."

"So, he isn't here now?" Ellen asked.

Erin shook her head as she coughed. "But he'll be here tonight. I guarantee it."

"Tell us about your symptoms," Tanya said.

"It's hard to breathe sometimes. I feel like I've got something caught in my lungs, and I can't cough it up."

"Any other symptoms?" Tanya asked. "Night terrors, upset stomach, fatigue?"

"I'm always exhausted, and sometimes dizzy, but no night terrors or nausea."

"Bad dreams?" Tanya asked.

"If I have them, I can't remember them," Erin said. "I don't feel like I sleep long enough to have dreams."

"Do you know anyone else with the Phantom Flu?" Sue asked. "Neighbors, friends, relatives?"

"We know dozens of families," Mary Jane said. "My sister-in-law and her two boys, many of Erin's old school mates, some of my co-workers…lots of people."

"Do they have anything in common?" Ellen asked.

Mrs. McGinty folded her arms and turned to her daughter. "I don't know. They're all from around here. Nobody in Las Vegas or any other surrounding area seems to be affected."

"We need to get to our next appointment," Tanya pointed out as she jumped to her feet.

Sue and Ellen got up, too, followed by Mary Jane, who said, "Thank you for coming by."

"If you think of anything the flu victims have in common," Ellen said, "you can tell us tonight."

"Okay," Erin said.

"We'll see you ladies this evening," Sue said as Mary Jane walked with them toward the door.

Out on the front stoop, Mrs. McGinty lowered her voice. "I hope you can help her. I've been on suicide watch for weeks. I don't know what else to do."

Ellen squeezed the woman's hand. "We'll do our best. See you to-night."

From the McGinty residence, Ellen, Sue, and Tanya took a cab to call on Pat and Kevin Blake—the older couple who had seen what they later believed was a ghost on the road on their way back to Boulder City from Las Vegas, and whose sister's father-in-law had been accidentally run over during a similar encounter.

The Mediterranean-style mansion sat on a hill overlooking Lake Mead. As Ellen and her friends entered through a gate near the curb, they came upon an expansive courtyard. Like the McGintys', the Blakes' yard was landscaped with pea gravel but also included sago palms, Texas sage, huge agave plants, blooming yucca, and an impressive fountain.

A woman in her seventies opened the front door. "Hello, there."

Before Ellen and her friends could respond, the door slammed shut.

The woman pulled it open again. "I'm sorry about that. My goodness! I have the back windows open. I suppose the wind did that. Come on in. I'm Pat, and this is my husband, Kevin."

Kevin was tall—nearly seven feet—and thick. He said hello and showed them through an elegant foyer and into a grand room with a wall of windows that faced Lake Mead.

"That view is breathtaking," Ellen said.

"We think so, too," Pat said as she followed them into the room. "Please have a seat, make yourselves comfortable. Kevin and I like to have an afternoon tea, so I hope you'll join us."

"That sounds lovely," Sue said.

"I'll be right back with the tea things," Pat said. "Dear, why don't you tell them what happened?"

Kevin cleared his throat. "If this had happened to someone else, and they'd told me about it, I'd think they were nuts. But it didn't happen to someone else. It happened to me."

"Start from the beginning," Sue said. "You were on your way home from Vegas, right?"

"That's right. We were just a few miles outside of town when I notice this young man on the side of the road. He can barely walk and keeps stumbling along, and as I creep up on him, I can see him in my headlights, and he falls smack-dab in the middle of the road."

"That must have given you a fright," Ellen said.

"Could Pat see him, too?" Tanya asked.

"She's the one who made me get out of the car to check on him," Kevin said. "I had rolled down my window to ask if I could call for an ambulance, worried it might be a trick and if I got out, he'd hit me over the head and steal my car."

Pat returned with a tray of what looked like cucumber sandwiches and butter cookies with a tea service for five and, as she sat it down on the coffee table, said, "I didn't think anyone could act that good. I was worried the man was in danger of dying."

"But he'd either run off or disappeared," Kevin said.

"This looks delicious," Sue said.

"Please help yourself," Pat said.

Sue thanked her as she took a sandwich. Ellen and Tanya each took one, too.

"No one who was dragging his feet and stumbling could have been in any shape to run," Pat said as she poured steaming water into five pretty cups, each with a tea bag.

"I didn't believe in ghosts, you see," Kevin said. "I thought the guy had run off after playing a stupid prank, until we got into town and heard that others had witnessed the very same thing."

Ellen took a cup from Pat. "Maybe he's pranked multiple people."

"What would be the point?" Pat asked.

"I don't know. For kicks?" Ellen wondered out loud.

"I suppose it's possible," Kevin said. "But if that's the case, this person should be charged with manslaughter, for what happened to Pat's sister-in-law's father."

"True," Ellen said.

"Given what else is going on around here, I think we should assume this is a ghost," Sue said.

"I agree," Tanya said. "What about the Phantom Flu? Obviously, the two of you don't have it."

"No." Pat sat down on the sofa beside her husband and took a sip of her tea. "Most of the people who live up here in the hills seem to be immune to it."

"Oh?" Ellen exchanged glances with her friends. "Do you have any thoughts about why?"

"Not really," Pat said.

"Maybe it spreads more easily in neighborhoods where the houses are closer together?" Kevin speculated.

"But they're saying it isn't contagious," Pat said.

"But if it really is a case of mass hysteria," he said, "maybe it spreads more easily where the masses are closer together."

"I see," Pat said before taking a sip of her tea.

"Has anything else out of the ordinary happened since you encountered that man, or ghost, on the road?" Ellen asked.

Pat and Kevin shook their heads.

"Did the ghost look familiar to you?" Sue asked.

"No," Kevin said.

While Ellen and her friends sipped their tea and ate the delicious sandwiches and cookies, they enjoyed the view of the lake and listened to the Blakes tell their story. They had retired to Boulder City from Michigan ten years ago, after Pat's brother and sister-in-law had moved there.

"We love it here," Pat said. "We enjoy driving into Vegas on the weekends and taking in the view when we're at home. Our neighbors are friendly. We've never regretted coming down here."

"Do you personally know anyone who's been affected by the Phantom Flu?" Sue asked them.

"Oh, sure," Pat said. "The woman from our dry cleaner, Tim from our favorite coffee shop, and a, oh, what's her name?" She turned to her husband. "That girl scout troop leader we always buy cookies from."

"Priscilla," Kevin said.

"That's right," Pat said. "Priscilla and both of her daughters came down with it."

They talked for a while about Las Vegas, retirement, and the Hoover Dam, and then Ellen and her friends said their goodbyes and took a cab back to their hotel.

During the cab ride, Brian called Ellen. He'd arranged for an early dinner with his cousin, the mayor of Boulder City.

"I told him about what you did for Mike," Brian said. "He's more than happy to meet with you."

Ellen hung up and turned to her friends. "Maybe this dinner with the mayor will help us to get at the bottom of the Phantom Flu."

"I'll tell you what the problem is," their cab driver said. "It's all those bodies buried beneath the dam. They're finally having their revenge."

"There aren't bodies buried beneath the dam," Sue said. "All the sources we've read…"

"Excuse my language, ma'am, but the hell there aren't," the cabby said. "I've heard stories about it my whole life. Until those bodies get a proper burial, our city is doomed."

CHAPTER SIX

Dinner with the Mayor

Ellen followed Sue and Tanya through the door of the Dillinger, where Brian had convinced them to meet him and the mayor for an early dinner of burgers and craft beer. At five o'clock, the pub-style restaurant had only a few other patrons, and most of them were at the bar.

Brian and his cousin were already seated at a table near a stage where Ellen supposed the restaurant offered live music on weekends. The men stood from their chairs as Ellen and her friends approached, and then Brian made introductions. After shaking hands, everyone took their seats.

Kiernan McManius was handsome, like his cousin, with white hair parted to one side. Unlike Brian, whose dark brows contrasted with gray eyes, Kiernan had white brows, like his hair, and crystal blue eyes. He was only slightly shorter than Brian and a little thicker around the middle.

"Brian's already making deals behind the bar." Kiernan chuckled. "My cousins have quite a knack for business."

"I told the manager I'd give them a good deal if the Dillinger wants to sell McManius beer."

"Look at you, doing your thing." Ellen smiled with admiration.

Brian winked. "Now it's time for you to do *your* thing. Sounds like Boulder City needs you."

"Why don't we order, and then Mayor McManius can tell us all about it?" Sue suggested.

"Please, call me Kiernan."

"Will do, Kiernan."

Without having to be asked, the mayor told them the town favorites on the menu, which Ellen could tell had endeared him to Sue. Then a cute girl in her twenties took their order and brought them their beer shortly after.

"Drink slowly, ladies," Ellen warned. "Don't forget we have an investigation to run tonight."

"Oh?" Kiernan asked. "Where?"

"Mary Jane McGinty's house," Sue replied. "Do you know the McGintys?"

"I knew Fred, Mary Jane's husband. That was year's ago."

"Her daughter has the Phantom Flu," Tanya explained.

"And has been visited by a ghost since mid-April," Ellen added.

"The McGintys aren't the only family dealing with that," Kiernan said somberly. "I can't tell you how many calls I get a day from people demanding that the city council do something."

"Damn," Brian said before taking a gulp of his beer.

The mayor shook his head. "It's been a disaster. With the doctors accusing an entire community of hallucinating and being psychosomatic, and all the paranormal investigators from around the nation swarming our city—I mean no offense, ladies, but not all of the ghost hunters are as professional in the way they conduct themselves as you. Anyway, it's been a nightmare."

"No offense taken," Sue said.

They were interrupted by the arrival of a young couple at their table. The young man was pointing his phone at them—whether to photograph or video, Ellen wasn't sure.

"Can we ask you a few questions, Mayor McManius?" the woman asked.

"I'd rather you make an appointment with my office," Kiernan said. "I'm trying to enjoy my evening with family and friends."

"Are the ladies of Ghost Healers, Inc. your relatives or friends?" the man asked as he recorded himself with his phone.

"Now's not the proper time for an interview," Sue said with her hands on her hips. "If you don't stop pestering the mayor, I'm going to call the cops on you two disrespectful fame seekers. If you really want attention, then do something positive with your lives. Karma can be a bitch if you act bitchy."

The young agitators frowned and fled the Dillinger.

Brian and Kiernan busted out laughing.

"No one messes with you, do they Mrs. Graham?" Kiernan said.

"You catch on fast, don't you?" she replied with a grin.

Everyone at the table laughed.

"So, what do you think of the beer?" Kiernan asked his cousin.

"Not bad. It's got a good flavor."

Ellen took a sip of her beer and nodded. "It is good." Then, turning to Kiernan, she asked, "In the museum at the Boulder Dam Hotel, a sign says that no bodies were buried beneath the dam. Is that true?"

The mayor shook his head. "That myth has been around for decades."

"Are you sure it's a myth?" Sue asked.

"Yes, I'm sure. It wasn't possible."

"Why not?" Tanya asked.

"The dam was built out of blocks, and concrete was delivered to the blocks in buckets. Each bucket only poured about two to six inches of concrete per block."

"Oh, I didn't know that," Sue said.

"While the men waited for the next bucket, they'd stomp on the concrete, to get the air pockets out. Then six more inches would be poured, and so on. The concrete firmed up as they packed it, so there was no way an entire body could be buried in it."

"I see," Ellen said.

"Some men drowned in the river, and their bodies were never recovered," Kiernan added, "but they aren't buried beneath the dam. They would have been swept away."

"That makes sense," Tanya said.

"I guess most people imagine 3.25 million cubic yards of concrete getting poured into a form all at once, with men slipping and drowning in it. But that's not how the dam was built." The mayor finished his beer and turned to his cousin. "You ready for another?"

"Sure, why not?"

Kiernan waved to their waitress.

"I wonder how the myth was started," Sue said.

"There was an earth dam up in Montana being built around the same time, where some men *were* buried alive and never found," the mayor said. "I suppose it's possible that people back then got confused about what happened at what dam."

"That makes a lot of dam sense," Sue said.

"That dam joke never gets old, does it?" Brian said with a laugh.

"Maybe a little," Ellen said with a laugh. "But seriously, Kiernan. Thanks for explaining that. But about the Phantom Flu—have you noticed any kind of pattern that might explain why some people and not others have come down with it?"

"The city council has been meeting every week for months, trying to find something—anything—to explain what's happening."

"Nothing?" Brian asked.

"Nada."

Just then their food arrived, along with Brian and Kiernan's beers. The burgers and fries looked delicious. As Ellen's plate was set in front of her, she hoped she wouldn't finish the fries. Losing twenty pounds after Paul's death had been easy, but keeping them off had seemed nearly impossible.

After condiments had been passed around the table and everyone had had a chance to sample their food, Ellen, asked the mayor, "Were the doctors able to pinpoint the original source?"

"That's usually a concern when dealing with a contagion," Kiernan said as he poured more ketchup on his hamburger. "We do know that the first patients to complain of the flu-like symptoms were among the elderly."

"How fast did it spread?" Brian asked before popping a fry into his mouth.

"By the end of April, two hundred people had reported symptoms. By the end of May, that number doubled. In June, another hundred or so fell ill. Fortunately, the numbers haven't changed since."

"That's bizarre," Sue said before taking a bite of her burger.

"Do you like it?" Brian asked Sue of the burger.

Sue nodded, giving Brian a thumbs up.

"Good. I'm glad you approve." Kiernan took a drink of his beer.

"How did the doctors initially respond to the epidemic?" Tanya asked.

"While they searched for a virus or bacteria in those who were sick, they also tested people who weren't, to see what they had in common that might have made them immune. That's back when they thought it was a contagion."

"Did they come up with anything?" Ellen asked.

"They had a few theories. Each one got shot down, eventually."

Ellen decided she should give Kiernan a chance to eat before asking her next question, but within a few minutes, something new had occurred to her.

"You said the flu began with the elderly," she said to Kiernan. "Is it possible that only people who were born here have been affected? Mary Jane McGinty, not originally from this area, isn't sick, but her daughter, *who was born here*, is."

"And the Blakes aren't from here," Sue added. "They're not sick."

"I was born here," Kiernan said. "And as you can see, I'm fine."

"Dam fine," Brian said as he clinked his beer bottle against his cousin's.

The ladies laughed. Both men were certainly fine, Ellen thought.

"Well, there's another theory shot down," Sue said.

"Yep," the mayor said. "I was born in the original Boulder Dam Hospital, so I'd say I'm as native as they come."

"What do you mean, 'original'?" Tanya asked.

"I don't know how much you ladies know about our town history," Kiernan said.

"Not a lot," Ellen admitted.

"And I'm sure I know even less," Brian added with a laugh.

"The first hospital was built in 1931 by Six Companies on a hilltop overlooking Lake Mead."

Sue lifted her brows. "I'd love to see it, if the building still exists."

"I'm afraid you're too late," Kiernan said.

"How long ago was the hospital replaced?" Ellen asked.

"The new hospital was built in the mid-seventies. For a while, the old building was used for church retreats, as it had breathtaking views of the lake; but then it sat vacant for years on a prime piece of property. Homeowners called it an eyesore and wanted it down. A developer by the name of Randy Schams is planning to build some upscale housing there."

"That's too bad," Tanya said. "That building was a piece of history you'll never get back."

"A group from the historical society tried to stop it, because the building had already been listed on the National Register of Historic Places."

"What?" Ellen gasped. "I can't believe it was allowed to be torn down after it was registered."

Kiernan's cheeks flushed. "My hands were tied. A young architect from this area wanted to turn the old hospital into a museum chronicling the Depression and Hoover Dam victims. He sought private support and government grants and lobbied my city council to intervene, but we had no legal jurisdiction to prevent the demolition."

"How sad," Tanya muttered.

Kiernan's face reddened even more. Ellen could tell he was embarrassed.

"We're not blaming you," she assured him.

"Schams was willing to sell it to the preservationists for a price, but neither they nor the city could afford it."

"That's too bad," Sue said. "I wished we'd known about it. *We* could have purchased it. In addition to being paranormal investigators, we've also become quite the preservationists ourselves, haven't we, ladies?"

Kiernan smiled. "You have something in common with my cousins, then."

"Indeed." Brian winked at Ellen.

"Well, the land hasn't been developed *yet*," Kiernan said. "You might be able to convince Randy to sell it to you, for the right price."

"How can we preserve something that's been demolished?" Ellen said, clutching her belly. The idea that something as significant as the hospital—where the builders of the Hoover Dam had been treated—being wiped from history was making her nauseated.

"From what I understand, Randy saved all the red roof tiles, windows, and bricks, planning to sell them to people wanting historical memorabilia."

Ellen's mouth fell open. Sue and Tanya's expressions of surprise mirrored her own.

"We need to look into this," Ellen said. "Don't you agree? This could be our next project."

"That's dam exciting!" Brian said with a laugh. "I don't suppose you'd let me turn it into something like my Kennedy School?"

"First, we need to see if the developer is still open to selling," Sue pointed out.

Kiernan's face returned to its natural color. "I can put you in touch."

"Wait a minute," Ellen said, as an idea struck her. "How long ago was the old hospital torn down?"

"End of February. Why?"

"End of February?" Ellen repeated. "Of this year?"

"Are you thinking what I'm thinking?" Sue asked her.

"That could explain *everything*," Tanya said.

Brian noticed the expressions on the faces of Ellen and her friends. "Wait, do you think that has something to do with the Phantom Flu?"

Ellen lifted her brows. "It dam well could."

Sue leaned closer to Kiernan. "What else can you tell us about the original hospital?"

"What do you want to know?" he asked.

"Did anything particularly violent ever occur there?" Tanya asked. "Like a mass murder?"

Kiernan's eyes widened. "No, I don't believe so. I've never heard of such a thing."

"Was a doctor ever convicted or suspected of malicious practices?" Sue asked.

The mayor shook his head. "I don't think so. You might want to talk to someone at the police department. Our chief of police has been around for almost as long as I have. Brent Needham is his name. He's got the flu, but nothing can slow that man down."

"Kiernan, can you think of *anything* strange that ever happened at the original hospital?" Ellen asked. "Anything at all?"

"Honestly, no, but we still have a few 31ers who might remember something from the early days, from before I was born."

"Thirty-one-ers?" Ellen asked.

"People who were living in 1931, when construction on the dam began."

"They can't have been old enough to remember much, could they have been?" Sue asked.

"One gentleman just turned 101," the mayor said. "One is ninety-nine, and another is in his mid-nineties, I believe."

"Oh, then maybe they might remember something," Tanya said. "Can you put us in touch with them?" She still had half a burger and most of her fries left on her plate, but she'd covered it with her napkin, a sign that she was done.

Although Ellen had less food left on her plate, she decided to follow Tanya's lead and quit, even if she wasn't yet full.

"The three I just mentioned live in a nursing home on the south side of town about ten minutes away," the mayor said, pulling a business card from his wallet. "I'll give you their names and the address, and you can visit them anytime you'd like." He pulled a pen from inside his jacket pocket and scribbled out a few names and an address on the back of the card before handing it to Sue, who was seated next to him.

"Thank you," Sue said, as she put the card into her purse.

"I can see the wheels spinning," Brian said. "What are you thinking, Ellen?"

Ellen took another sip of her beer. "I'm thinking that the ghosts that have been haunting this town may have been people who died at the original hospital and, for whatever reason, weren't able to find peace. When the building was demolished, they scattered, no longer having the familiar place that tethered them."

"That's a sound theory," Brian said.

When Kiernan made no comment, Ellen realized he was a skeptic. She understood how he felt. It hadn't been that long ago when she was one, too.

"That still doesn't explain why over five hundred people are experiencing flu-like symptoms," Tanya pointed out.

"Did Boulder City ever suffer from a flu epidemic?" Sue asked the mayor.

"Not that I know of, but maybe the 31ers will know differently."

After dinner, Kirk drove Ellen, Brian, Sue, and Tanya back to the Boulder Dam Hotel, where they decided to rest for an hour, to recharge their batteries before the investigation at the McGinty residence.

Brian, who had moved into Ellen's room for the night, took her into his arms as soon as they were behind closed doors.

"I'm so glad to see you," Ellen whispered into his neck. "I wish you didn't have to leave in the morning."

He stroked her hair. "I'll come back next weekend, if you still want to go to Vegas."

"Let's see how the investigation is going before we make plans—though, you could still come here, even if we don't go to Vegas."

Inwardly, she chastised herself, remembering that she'd meant to put a little distance between them, just until she'd felt better about Paul. Her stomach clenched as she imagined Paul looking down at her, wondering if she'd already forgotten him and their thirty years together.

"What's wrong?" Brian asked, picking up on her mood.

"Nothing. I'm just thinking about the hospital being demolished."

"Come here, you busy bee." He covered her mouth with his, sending her into the clouds.

CHAPTER SEVEN

A Paranormal Investigation

Kirk drove Ellen and her friends to the McGinty residence just before dusk, where both Kirk and Brian helped to set up the full-spectrum cameras, passive infrared motion detectors, the big EMF recorder, and their new electromagnetic pump in the living room. Once the equipment was in place, Kirk left to wait in the limo.

Mary Jane offered everyone homemade brownies. Ellen was about to take one, after Sue and Brian, but when Tanya said, "No thanks," Ellen decided to do the same. She'd never keep her weight off if she didn't make some sacrifices.

Erin sat, half-asleep, in the recliner as though she hadn't moved from it all day. She wore the same pajamas and quilt, and her long hair lay piled over her head on the back of the recliner like a bird's nest. Ellen felt sorry for the girl. Dark circles beneath her eyes and a face full of acne indicated how stressed she'd been.

Erin's mother sat on the sofa facing the back of the room, on the end nearest her daughter. Brian took a seat on the other end of it. Ellen and her friends remained standing in the middle of the room, around the coffee table. Tanya had a thermometer, Sue an EMF detector, and Ellen an audio recorder. The full-spectrum cameras were situated on tripods in three corners of the room.

Ellen pulled a notepad from one of the bags, along with a pencil. "Before we begin, we need to take some baseline readings."

"It's seventy-six degrees," Tanya said.

Sue put on her readers and studied her EMF detector. "I'm picking up 2.23 milliGauss. That's with the electromagnetic pump on. It was only 1.22 milliGauss before."

Ellen made notes and laid the pad and pencil on the coffee table.

"What does that mean?" Erin asked, in between coughs.

"It's very hard for most ghosts to maneuver on a frequency that we can see and hear," Ellen explained. "They need energy, like electricity."

Sue looked up from her EMF detector. "When they feed on electricity, they radiate electromagnetic radiation that our instruments can measure. They also feed on heat, which is another kind of energy. So, if a room suddenly gets chilly, that's a sign."

"It's also a sign if your phone dies." Tanya sat directly across from Mary Jane, on the couch facing the front of the house, so that Erin and her recliner were between them. "That's happened to us a lot."

"That's why we broke down and bought that new box over there." Ellen pointed to the electromagnetic pump near the front door. "It creates electromagnetic radiation that can be used by spirits."

Brian sat back and crossed one leg over the other. "Fascinating stuff, isn't it?"

"Why, yes," Mary Jane said nervously.

Erin coughed and cleared her throat. "The other ghost hunters had something they called a ghost box. They said the spirits can talk to them on it. Do you have one?"

"Ellen doesn't believe in those," Sue said.

"I never said I didn't believe in them." Blood rushed to Ellen's cheeks. "I just don't think they're very accurate."

"Why not?" Erin asked.

"A ghost, or spirit, box is basically a radio that continuously scans through channels," Ellen said. "Some paranormal investigators believe that ghosts can use the white noise to formulate words."

"But you disagree?" Erin asked.

"I think it's easy to make nonsense into whatever you want it to be," Ellen said. "It's just not precise enough for me."

"Should I make the circle?" Tanya asked from the couch.

"I'll do it." Sue reached into one of their bags and brought out a shaker of salt. "This will vacuum right up, Mary Jane. I hope you don't mind. It's our protection."

"I've tried salt," Erin said, "but it didn't stop the ghost from coming."

Erin broke into another coughing fit.

Ellen waited until the fit was over before saying, "We're not trying to stop him from coming."

"The salt will create a barrier," Sue explained as she sprinkled a white line around the perimeter of the room, "so the spirit can't attach to or possess any of us."

Tanya crossed her arms over her lap. "And you don't want that to happen. It's miserable."

"You sound like you're speaking from experience," Mrs. McGinty said.

Tanya raised her brows and nodded but said no more about it.

Erin sighed. "I thought you were here to stop the ghost from bothering me."

Ellen could tell that Erin was anxious to move on with her life. "To do that, we need to find out why he's here."

"Banishing a ghost with a smudge stick won't get rid of it forever," Sue said as she continued to pour salt. "You have to find out what's keeping the spirit from moving on."

"And how will you do that?" Erin asked.

"By communicating with it." With the circle complete, Sue placed the saltshaker back into the bag. "Ready?"

Ellen and Tanya nodded. Sue switched off the floor lamp. The dim purple glow of the full-spectrum cameras and the filtered light from a streetlamp afforded the only light in the otherwise darkened room.

"I'm scared, Mom," Erin whispered.

Mary Jane McGinty reached out to hold her daughter's hand.

Ellen wanted to reassure Erin, but one never knew what might happen when attempting to talk with the dead.

"Stay in the circle of salt," Tanya reminded them as Sue took a seat beside her. "No matter what happens, don't break the circle."

Ellen, the only one to remain standing, pushed *play* on her handheld audio recorder and took a deep breath. "Spirits of the other realm, we mean you no harm. We're here to help you to find peace. Please use the energy from our electromagnetic pump to communicate with us. Appear to us. Talk to us. We want to help."

"The temperature has dropped to seventy degrees," Tanya whispered. "Make that sixty-nine."

"What was that?" Brian asked, turning toward the front door.

Ellen glanced around but saw nothing. "Did you hear something?"

"I thought I felt someone walking behind me, behind the couch, by the front window."

Mary Jane glanced over her shoulder. "I felt something, too."

"The EMF detector is all over the place," Sue said.

Tanya studied her temperature gauge. "Sixty-five degrees."

"Is someone there?" Sue asked. "Can you give us a sign?"

When nothing happened, Ellen said again, "Spirits of the other realm, we come in peace. If anyone is here with us, please give us a sign."

Erin's eyes widened. She stared across the room, toward the front window, behind Ellen, and trembled as she pulled her quilt up to her face. "Please, leave me alone. Stop tormenting me. Please! I can't take it anymore."

Mary Jane jumped from the couch and huddled beside Erin, with her arms protectively around her daughter. She shook life a leaf in the wind as she stared in terror at something behind the sofa.

Ellen turned to see a tall, thin, transparent shape hovering next to the front window. Brian saw it, too, and gasped. Although the blinds were drawn, the light from the street seeped through the cracks, giving the appearance of stripes on the specter.

Ellen's skin broke out with goosebumps, and the hair on the back of her neck stood up. As often as she'd seen a ghost, it was never less than terrifying. "Who are you? What's your name?"

The figure seemed to be speaking, but Ellen heard no sound coming from his mouth. She wondered if the sound of her own heart pounding in her ears was getting in the way.

"Can you hear him?" she asked Erin and the others.

Erin cowered beneath her quilt and shook her head. Mary Jane did the same.

"Maybe the instruments are picking it up," Sue said. "Keep talking to him."

"Why are you here?" Ellen asked, trying to keep from shaking. Her knees were so wobbly, that she had to grab onto the arm of the sofa. "Do you have a message for us?"

The apparition flickered a few times before stabilizing again. When he raised his arms and swung them angrily, Ellen jumped back and bumped into the coffee table.

"Oh, spirit of the other realm," Sue began. "We come in peace. We mean you no harm. If you understand, could you knock on the wall behind you?"

The figure raised a long, thin arm, and when he brought it down, his hand seemed to pass through the wall beside the window, making no sound.

"That's incredible," Brian whispered, unable to peel his eyes from the specter.

"Maybe we should use the Ouija Board," Tanya whispered. "Want to?"

"Wait, aren't those evil?" Erin asked. "I heard Ouija Boards invite the evil in."

"I don't want to invite the evil in," Mrs. McGinty said nervously.

"We won't do anything without your permission," Ellen began. "It's just that the Ouija Board gives us the most effective form of communication, in our experience—as long as you trust the people who are using it."

"And I don't mean to frighten you," Sue said. "But the evil may already be in."

Clearly shaken, but also desperate, Mary Jane said, "Okay, then. Go ahead."

Tanya pulled the board from one of the bags and laid it on the coffee table between the two couches. Ellen sat beside Brian on one couch. Sue sat beside Tanya on the other. Ellen and her friends put their instruments on the coffee table and gently touched their fingers to the planchette. Brian kept his eyes on the specter behind them, as did Mary Jane and her daughter.

Ellen glanced over her shoulder to look at it again. He was standing very still, looking more like a thin ray of light than a man. Erin put the quilt over her head, unable to watch. Mary Jane continued to protectively embrace her daughter. Brian stared at the figure, as though paralyzed with fear. Ellen realized it was the first time he'd ever seen a ghost.

"Spirit of the other realm," Sue began, "can you move the planchette?"

Ellen felt the plastic indicator beneath her fingers pulse an inch away from her, toward Sue, before stopping.

"Spirit," Ellen began, "if that's you moving the planchette, please move it to the word YES on the board."

In a series of jerky starts and stops, the planchette carried their fingers toward the word YES.

"That's amazing," Mrs. McGinty whispered.

"Can you spell out your name?" Sue asked the ghost.

The planchette moved abruptly before stopping on the letter J.

"J," Tanya said.

The planchette continued to spell A-M-E-S.

"James?" Sue asked.

The planchette moved to YES.

"That was the name of Fred's grandfather," Mary Jane muttered with tears in her eyes.

"James?" Ellen began. "Are you Erin's ancestor? Are you James McGinty?"

The planchette circled around the board and returned to YES.

Mary Jane broke into tears. Erin lifted her head from the quilt to peek across the room at the figure, still hovering by the front window.

"Why are you haunting me?" Erin asked with trembling lips, as tears and snot ran down her face. "How could you do this to me, if you're my great-grandfather?"

The planchette began to move again. Erin watched eagerly as it spelled out L-O-S-T.

"You're lost?" Tanya asked.

The planchette circled to YES.

"What year did you die," Sue asked.

The planchette moved to 1-9-3-2.

"That's incredible," Mary Jane said.

"Do you have a message for us?" Tanya asked.

The planchette spelled G-A-S.

When it stopped moving, Brian said, "Gas? What does that mean? Could he be warning you of a gas leak?"

"I don't know," Mary Jane said. "I do have a gas stove."

Brian jumped to his feet.

"Don't break the circle," Sue warned.

Brian ran his fingers through his silver hair. "Even if it means we may all be exposed to carbon monoxide poisoning?"

"What was that?" Erin asked, still peeking over the top of her quilt. "I heard something outside."

Ellen looked behind her to see that the ghost had vanished.

Mary Jane stood upright. "I think there's someone at the door."

"Don't break the circle," Tanya said.

The doorbell rang.

"Are you expecting someone?" Brian asked Mary Jane.

"No, but shouldn't I go and see who it is?"

"I don't think you should break the circle just yet," Tanya said. "Should we turn on the lamp?"

"If we do, whoever's at the door will know someone's home," Sue whispered. "Let's wait until they go away."

"Hello?" the voice of a young man called through the door. "Mary Jane McGinty? Are you at home? We're paranormal investigators. We'd like to talk to you about your comment on the Ghost Healers blog. Can we have a few minutes of your time?"

Erin frowned at her mother. "I told you not to post about this on the internet."

Brian put his finger to his lips.

"Hello?" the young man asked again. "Is anyone home?"

Ellen and the others waited in silence for at least three minutes before they heard a group of people climb into a car parked outside.

"They're going to wait out there," Mary Jane said. "This has happened before."

Erin clutched fistfuls of her messy hair. "I told you not to post about this. This isn't your story to tell!"

In the next moment, someone knocked on the door. "I hear you in there. Please answer the door. I want to help you."

"I'll handle this," Brian said. "Turn on the lamp."

Tanya, who was closest to the floor lamp, switched on the light.

Brain stepped from the circle, went to the door, and opened it. "Mrs. McGinty isn't interested in talking with you. Please leave, or we'll call the cops."

"Are you Mr. McGinty?" the young man asked.

Ellen climbed to her feet and stood beside Brian. The young man at the door wore skinny jeans and a t-shirt and had silver studs on his earlobes and on one nostril. Two other men in similar attire hung back at the end of the flagstone path near the curb.

"I need you to leave," Brian said to the young man. "Get out of here. Now."

The young men turned away, making rude comments, as they climbed into a vehicle that was parked on the curb. Brian stood there at the door until he saw them drive away.

From the limo in the driveway, Kirk waved at Brian, as if checking to make sure all was okay. Brian waved back.

"Geez Louise," Ellen said, returning to her seat. "Just when we were on to something."

"Should we try again?" Sue asked.

Brian headed for the kitchen. "I'm going to check that stove."

"I don't think I can take this anymore," Erin said. "I can't believe my own great-grandfather would torment me."

"He may be tormented, too," Ellen said gently. "Mary Jane, what do you know about James?"

"Not much. Only that he helped to build the dam."

Ellen, Sue, and Tanya straightened their backs, all at the same time.

"Did he die tragically?" Tanya asked. "Was he killed on the job?"

"No, not at all. Fred told me that his father died of pneumonia."

The bulb in the floor lamp flickered. Ellen and the others glanced around the room, looking for the ghost, but he was nowhere to be found.

"I think he's still here," Erin groaned.

Maybe we should redo the circle," Tanya said.

"Wait for Brian," Sue said.

Ellen cocked her head to the side. "By any chance, did Fred pass away at the old Boulder City Hospital?"

"I'm not sure," Mary Jane said. "It's possible. Why do you ask?"

"I bet we can find records," Sue said.

"It's just a theory," Ellen said to Mrs. McGinty. "We've just learned that the old hospital was torn down in February, just before the symptoms and paranormal sightings began."

"Sometimes ghosts get connected to a place," Sue explained. "The demolition could be the reason so many sightings have been reported."

Erin wiped her red, swollen eyes. "But why would he come here?"

"We don't know, yet," Ellen said. "He may need help, or he may want to warn you about something. I promise you that we won't stop investigating until we figure this out. Okay?"

Erin tried to smile, but she didn't seem to believe Ellen.

"It's not the stove," Brian said as he returned to the living room. "I didn't see any signs of a leak."

"Maybe we should pack up and let the McGintys rest," Tanya said.

Sue took the shaker of salt from her bag and handed it to Erin. "Put this around you when you go to sleep at night. It won't stop him from coming to you, but as long as you don't break the circle, he won't be able to hurt you, okay?"

"Thank you," Erin said as she took the shaker from Sue.

Brian called Kirk back inside to help load up the equipment.

After they had said their goodbyes to the McGintys and had climbed into the back of the limo, Brian said, "That was scary as hell. I don't know how you ladies do it."

"It's a calling," Sue said. "We feel like it's our purpose to help the spirits who, for one reason or another, can't move on."

"You ladies have some big balls—that's all I'm saying. I've never been so spooked in my life. I think I'm still shaking."

"You've told us that before," Sue said. "Remember? Do you remember what I said after?"

Brian's cheeks turned red. "I remember. You reminded me that you have breasts—as if I need reminding."

Ellen shook her head as Tanya rolled her eyes.

Sue laughed. "It's just that I know a man with big balls, and he's a coward."

"Is he someone you dated?" Tanya asked.

"Yes," Sue said. "And now I'm married to him."

Everyone laughed. Ellen knew Sue was only making a joke. Her husband was no coward.

Ellen asked, "Would y'all mind if we made a quick stop at the site of the old hospital? I'd love to check it out."

"Why don't we go after breakfast tomorrow?" Tanya said, stifling a yawn.

"I'm dying to see it, too," Sue said. "You can wait in the limo, Tanya. Okay? That all right with you, Brian?"

"I don't mind. Where is it?" Brian asked.

"Aren't you guys exhausted?" Tanya asked. "It's been a long day."

Ellen chuckled. They'd nearly died in a plane crash the previous night and had spent all day trying to talk to the dead. "That's an understatement."

"I'm Googling it now," Sue said to Brian as she put on her readers and tapped on her phone. "Oh, it's only a few minutes from our hotel, at 701 Park Place."

"Do you mind, Tanya?" Ellen asked.

"Does it matter?" she asked.

"Not really," Sue teased.

"I don't care," Tanya said. "I'm going to sleep."

Tanya closed her eyes and leaned against the window beside her.

Brian rolled down the window between the front and back of the limo to give Kirk the address.

"Maybe we can pick up on an emotion or something that could help us solve this mystery," Ellen said.

"I'm also curious to see what they've done," Sue said. "If the developer really hasn't started yet, we just might have a chance at convincing him to let us buy it."

"Don't let him know how eager we are," Tanya warned, keeping her eyes closed. "You might drive up the price."

"It's probably too late, anyway," Sue said.

"We'll find out soon enough," Brian said, looking at his phone. "Kiernan just texted me Randy's number."

CHAPTER EIGHT

The Old Boulder City Hospital Grounds

Kirk pulled the limo up to a curb at the base of a hill. About five yards from the curb, a six-foot high fence circled the perimeter of the property. Brian helped Ellen and her friends—including Tanya, who didn't want to be left behind—from the limo and then followed them up the hillside to the fence, using their phones to illuminate their path.

From the side of the hill, the bright lights of Las Vegas shone in the west and the dark void that was Lake Mead sat eerily still in the east. Ellen shined her flashlight app on a fence made of PVC piping lined with blue opaque plastic. More than one "No Trespassing" sign was taped to the outside of the plastic.

"Shall we break the law?" Sue asked.

"Definitely," Ellen said. "Let's see if we can find a gate or an opening. I don't want to trespass *and* vandalize all in one night."

"I agree," Sue said. "We should save *something* for another time."

As Brian followed Ellen and her friends, he said, "I could just call Randy Schams and get permission. Then we wouldn't have to break any laws."

"Oh, you're no fun," Sue teased.

"It's already after ten," Tanya said. "Isn't it too late to call?"

Ellen turned back to Brian, who was trailing behind her. "And what if he says no?"

Brian caught up to her and pecked her on the cheek. "Nothing's gonna stop you, huh?"

"Now, Brian, no distracting Ellen," Sue said. "We need her focused."

"I haven't been scolded since the three of you were in Portland," Brian said grinning.

"Are you guys sure we shouldn't wait and come back in the morning?" Tanya said. "Maybe Randy would agree to meet us here."

"We should definitely come in the morning," Ellen said. "But I'd still like to check out the place tonight."

Ellen led the group along the perimeter of the PVC and plastic, searching for an opening. As they rounded the fence to the west, towards the lights of Las Vegas, Ellen found what she was looking for: a three-foot gap.

"It's not very secure." Ellen stepped inside and shined her light all around the job site.

"What the hell?" Brian said from behind her.

"What?" Tanya shined her light around, too.

Sue struggled to catch up and, panting, asked, "What do you see?"

The first thing Ellen noticed was a long set of concrete steps—at least two dozen in the hillside. To the left, at the top of the hill, a tree billowed in the nighttime breeze and made shadows on piles of bricks beneath it.

"Did you see something?" Ellen whispered to Brian.

"I must have imagined it," he said, as he rubbed his eyes. "I'm probably still freaking out after seeing that ghost at the McGinty house."

"What do you think you saw just now?" Sue asked him.

"Guys," Tanya said. "Let's go back. I have a bad feeling."

"Brian? What did you see?" Ellen asked again.

Brian looked embarrassed and reluctant, but Ellen squeezed his shoulder and said, "It's okay. You can trust us."

"I thought I saw someone on the other side of those bricks."

"A person?" Sue asked.

"There could be a vagrant up there," Tanya whispered.

"No. I don't think it was a person. It was more of a shadow."

"A shadow person?" Sue asked.

"I think so. Maybe I just imagined it. It didn't look anything like the ghost we saw at the McGinty house. It was like a silhouette."

"There are different kinds of specters," Ellen said. "They're basically energy, but they can appear differently."

"We've seen a shadow person before," Tanya said. "In Tulsa."

Sue folded her arms across her chest against the chilly breeze. "The one in Tulsa wasn't malevolent, but I'm getting a bad feeling."

"Like what? What kind of feeling?" Ellen asked, disappointed that she felt nothing.

"Regret, fear, anger," Sue said.

"Let's go back," Tanya said again.

Ellen shined her light on the top of the steps. "I'm just going to have a quick look, and then we can go."

"Then I'm going with you," Brian said, taking her hand.

His hand was clammy and trembling. She'd never seen Brian this afraid before.

"We don't have to do this, if you don't want to," she whispered.

"I'd never want to hold you back."

Ellen took a deep breath. With her light in one hand and Brian's hand in the other, she led him up the concrete steps. The closer she got to the hilltop, the more uneasy she felt, but she'd gone too far to turn back now.

When they reached the top, they found a cement slab in the shape of an L surrounded by rock and gravel.

"This looks like the original slab for the hospital," Ellen whispered.

"The developers haven't made much progress in six months."

"Maybe all the workers got the Phantom Flu."

Ellen glanced back at Sue and Tanya waiting at the bottom of the steps.

"What do you see?" Sue called out.

Brian stiffened beside her. "Oh, my God."

Ellen glanced around. "What is it?"

He shined his light in the corner of the slab, where the two sides of the L met.

"What is that?" She took a few steps closer with her light and gasped.

A mutilated body was sprawled in a pool of blood.

Ellen screamed.

"What's wrong?" Sue cried from below.

"Ellen?" Tanya shouted. "Oh, my God, Ellen. Are you okay?"

Tanya soon reached the top of the steps and was at Ellen's side. "Oh, my God. Is that a body?"

"There's writing in the blood." Ellen took a few shaky steps closer.

In her circle of light appeared a message: *I did as I was told.*

"Is everything okay up there?" Sue called out. "Do I need to come up there? I'd rather not, unless you need me."

"Don't come up!" Brian shouted.

"Let's get out of here!" Tanya dashed back down the concrete steps.

Ellen moved closer to the body to look for clues.

"What are you doing?" Brian said from behind her. "We need to leave. We could be in danger."

She pointed her phone at the horrible sight. "I'm just going to take a quick photo."

"Don't do that!" Brian said, grabbing her hand. "If anyone finds out we were here . . . come on, let's go."

Brian pulled her away, but not before she snapped her picture. She followed him down the concrete steps to find Sue waiting at the bottom, perplexed.

Tanya was nowhere to be seen.

"What's going on?" Sue cried as they reached her.

"I'll explain in the limo," Brian said. "Come on."

Brian grabbed Sue's hand and half-dragged her through the opening in the fence and down the side of the hill as Ellen hurried beside him.

Before they reached the limo, the three young ghost hunters that had been at the McGinty's met them in the grass on the hillside, their car parked behind the limo.

"We just want to ask you a few questions," the young man who'd been at the door said again.

Brian groaned. "Now's not a good time. We need to call the cops. We saw something disturbing up there."

"Really?" another young man said with a look of excitement. "Was it a ghost?"

The three young men started running up the hill.

"Stay away from there!" Brian shouted.

But the young people ignored him.

"Stop!" Ellen cried. "Come back! We'll talk to you!"

"It's no use," Brian said.

"What do we do now?" Ellen wondered out loud.

"We have no choice but to call the police, now that we've been seen."

Sue put her hands on her hips. "Will someone please explain to me what the heck is going on?"

"Let's get in the limo. We'll talk there." Brian crossed the lawn and opened the car door.

Ellen followed Sue inside, where Tanya was curled in her seat like a baby giraffe.

"We found a dead body up there," Ellen said to Sue, handing over her phone. "Take a look."

"What?" Sue put on her readers and inspected the photo. "Oh, my God! How terrible! Is that writing in the blood?"

"It says, *I did as I was told,*" Ellen said.

"What could that mean?" Sue wondered. "Do you think this is related to the Phantom Flu and the paranormal sightings?"

"I have no idea," Ellen said, still trembling and probably in shock.

"Tanya?" Brian asked. "Are you okay?"

Tanya cringed and shook her head. "I just need a minute."

"Why haven't we already called 9-1-1?" Sue wanted to know.

Brian took out his phone. "I'm calling now, but you ladies do realize that you'll be prime suspects."

Ellen gasped. "What makes you say that, Brian?"

"You just told my cousin, *the mayor*, how badly you want this property," Brian said. "And don't you think finding a mutilated body with a foreboding message written in blood will drive down the price? No one's going to want to buy a house up there once they find out about this."

"I hadn't thought of that," Ellen said.

"Brian's right," Sue said. "We have a motive. And we're also paranormal investigators, so that makes us doubly suspect."

"How so?" Ellen asked.

"They'll think we set it up to look like we'd been interacting with ghosts, to boost our notoriety as paranormal investigators."

Tanya began to cry. "Can we please just go back to the hotel?"

Brian dialed 9-1-1. "We need to wait for the cops to arrive, so we can give them statements."

"If we leave, it will make us look guilty," Sue said to Tanya.

At that moment, Ellen noticed the three young people running down the side of the hill. One of them took a photo of the limo and then followed the others back into their car before screeching away.

"I hope they didn't tamper with the crime scene," Ellen said. "I'm glad I took my photo."

She glanced over at Brian, who was giving a report of what they found to the 9-1-1 dispatcher. Sue comforted a sobbing Tanya.

"I wish we would have waited to come in the morning," Tanya muttered through her tears. "What if we get arrested? Tried for murder? Indicted? Oh, God. I want to go back to San Antonio."

"I'm sorry," Ellen said, patting her friend's hand. "I won't let us get arrested."

Tanya rolled her eyes. "Like you have any control over this."

It was after midnight when they finally arrived at their hotel, exhausted from long interviews at the scene of the crime. Ellen had had to tell her story three times—all of them had—once to each of the three officers. Although Ellen and her friends hadn't been charged, they'd been asked to report to the police department the following morning to answer more questions—all but Brian, who was allowed to return to Portland, so long as he remained available by phone, in case the Boulder City Police needed to reach him.

The hotel lobby was dark and vacant, as it had been the previous night, when Ellen, Sue, and Tanya had first arrived in Boulder City. A lamp on the front desk and a dim fixture over the stairs provided just enough light for them to find their way toward the elevator. As they waited for the elevator to make its way down from the upper level, a young woman called to them from the lobby.

"Don't give up," she chirped. "Sometimes you have to go through the darkness to get to the light."

Ellen and her friends glanced at one another in surprise. Ellen turned back toward the lobby, looking for the woman, but found no one there.

"Hello?" Sue called out. "Are you there?"

The four of them stood in the lobby in silence for many minutes but heard nothing more.

"Y'all heard that, right?" Ellen asked.

"Sometimes you have to go through the darkness to get to the light?" Sue repeated.

"Do you think someone is playing a trick on us?" Ellen whispered.

"The voice was so clear," Sue said.

"Last night, we thought we were talking to a living person," Tanya said. "That's rare, isn't it? For a ghost to speak with such clarity?"

"Maybe that's why we can't see her," Ellen speculated. "She uses her energy to be heard. James McGinty uses his energy to be seen. Maybe most ghosts can't manage both."

"I'm going to bed," Tanya said as she turned back toward the elevator.

The others followed.

As Brian held the elevator door, he said, "You haven't told me about the ghost from last night."

Ellen told him the details as they rode the elevator to their floor and headed to their rooms. Tanya said goodnight and disappeared behind her door. Sue did the same. Once Ellen and Brian were alone in their room, Brian took her into his arms.

"What a day," he said.

"What time do you leave in the morning?"

"Too early."

"Let's go to bed."

They undressed and crawled beneath the covers and kissed each other good night. Ellen turned out the lamp and lay beside Brian and finally allowed herself to feel afraid. She'd put up a good show for the others— even for Brian. But now that everything was quiet, she could admit to herself how terrified she'd been—and still was. She took a deep breath and tried to calm her nerves. Tears pricked her eyes as she recalled how safe she used to feel in Paul's arms. Even if they hadn't always gotten along, even if they didn't enjoy doing the same things, he'd been there for her, for thirty years. He'd been the constant in her life that had grounded her and had made her feel safe and secure. As grateful as she was to have Brian by her side, she felt, for the first time since he'd passed, that she needed Paul.

She turned on her side with her back to Brian and allowed her tears to fall.

CHAPTER NINE

Questioning

Ellen was exhausted when the alarm on her phone woke her. She remembered Brian kissing her goodbye before dawn. That had been three hours ago, though it seemed as if only a few minutes had passed. The room had still been dark and quiet, and now light filtered through the tops of the curtains, and she could hear noises in the room next door. She groaned and reset the alarm, so she could sleep for fifteen more minutes, but, just as she had drifted back to sleep, the alarm sounded again.

"Oh, hell," she said, as she yawned and stretched.

After a quick shower, she dressed and got ready to meet her friends for breakfast downstairs. On the way, she met Sue in the hallway.

"Good morning," Sue said. "I hope you slept better than I did."

"I doubt it. Have you seen Tanya yet this morning?"

"She's sleeping in. She said to text her back when we're ready to go to the station, and she'll meet us in the lobby."

As they waited for the elevator, Ellen said, "She was pretty mad last night."

"Do you blame her?"

"No."

When they reached the restaurant, they were seated right away. Sue ordered the Big Dam Breakfast and coffee. Ellen, whose stomach still churned with fear and dread over what had happened the night before, wanted something light, so she ordered coffee and a blueberry yogurt parfait.

While they waited for their food to arrive, Sue said, "I'm going to tell you something, but I need you to promise not to say anything to Tanya. She's already so upset, and I think this will only make her feel worse."

"I promise. What is it?"

Sue waited as the waitress served their coffee. They thanked her, and after each of them had taken a few sips, Sue leaned forward and said, "Something happened to me last night."

"Oh, no. Tell me."

"Well, when I couldn't fall asleep, I went looking for a vending machine, hoping to find a snack—you know, some comfort food."

"Did you find one?"

"Not on our floor, so I came downstairs."

"Did you hear the ghost again?"

"Oh, yes."

Ellen's arms broke out in goosebumps. "Oh my gosh. What did she say? What happened?"

"I was bending over the machine, waiting for my Ding Dongs to fall into the dispenser, when I thought I felt someone standing behind me. When I looked, there was no one there."

"But you felt her?"

"Yes, but for only a second, and then I didn't feel her anymore. So, I said, 'Is someone there?' I stood there for a few minutes, just listening. It got so cold that I got chills. Again, I said, 'I mean you no harm. If you're there, please feel free to give me a sign.'"

"That was brave of you."

"Or stupid. Anyway, I was about to give up when I felt someone standing right beside me. I couldn't see anything, but I could sense it. It was like she was inches from me. And then, right beside my left ear, I heard a whisper in the same disembodied young woman's voice we heard last night."

"Oh my gosh! What did she say?"

Their breakfast arrived, so Sue stopped telling her story until the waitress had served them and left the table.

Then Sue leaned forward. "She said, 'He followed you here.'"

Ellen waited, thinking there would be more, but when Sue began to salt her eggs, Ellen asked, "Was that it? *He followed you here?*"

"That was it. I got so scared that I ran to the elevator without my Ding Dongs!"

Ellen chuckled. "You must have been pretty scared to leave those behind."

"Heck, yeah, I was! I could feel her breath on my ear—that's how close she was!"

"Who do you think she was talking about?" Ellen asked before she took a bite of the blueberry yogurt parfait.

"I hope I'm wrong, but I think she might have been referring to the shadow man Brian saw at the old hospital grounds last night."

A chill crept down Ellen's spine. "Oh, God. I hope not. Brian wasn't even sure if he saw anything."

"I felt it, though. I felt the evil. Tanya did, too."

Ellen's stomach did a flipflop at the thought of a malicious spirit following them from the crime scene. "Maybe we should all sleep in the same room tonight inside a circle of protection."

"I was thinking the very same thing," Sue said. "But how do we manage it without alarming Tanya?"

Tanya was suddenly standing beside their table. "What are you guys talking about?"

"I thought you were going to sleep in," Ellen said, trying to hide how startled she was.

Tanya pulled out a chair and sat down. "I couldn't sleep, so I decided to come down."

"Do you want to order something?" Sue asked.

"I think I'll just have some coffee. So, what did you mean about managing something without alarming me?"

Ellen looked to Sue for help.

Sue said, "We feel bad for making you go to the hospital grounds last night."

"Well, you should."

"I know." Sue's cheeks turned pink. "And we were really shaken up by it, too. So, we were thinking…"

"We should sleep in one room, inside a circle of protection, just until our nerves are less rattled," Ellen finished.

"That's a good idea," Tanya said. "Sue has the king-size bed. Why don't we sleep there? We can go over the data we collected from the McGinty investigation there, too. Sound good?"

"Sounds perfect," Sue said.

Relieved that Tanya seemed satisfied, Ellen and her friends finished their breakfast in relative peace, until it was time to go to the station for questioning.

Kirk was waiting in the limo in front of the hotel, Brian having asked his driver to take care of Ellen and her friends in his absence. When they arrived at the Boulder City Police Department, they were taken directly to the conference room down the hall on the first floor, where the mayor and Chief Brent Needham were already waiting.

Chief Needham appeared to be in his late sixties—around Kiernan's age—though he was thicker and bald and had dark brown eyes. He also had dark circles under his eyes and a persistent cough. Ellen remembered Kiernan mentioning that the chief suffered from the Phantom Flu.

"Can I get you ladies anything to drink?" Kiernan asked once they'd been introduced. "Coffee? Soda?"

"None for me, thanks," Sue said as she took her seat at the long conference table beside Tanya. "I just had the Big Dam Breakfast."

"Oh, that's my favorite place to eat," Chief Needham said. "It's dam good, isn't it?"

"*Dam* good," Sue repeated.

Ellen, who sat on the other side of Sue, also declined, but Tanya said, "I'll take some coffee, if you don't mind, with a little cream and sugar."

As the mayor turned to a sideboard and poured Tanya a cup, Ellen said to the chief, "I'm surprised you aren't interrogating us in separate rooms—or will you be taking us back, one at a time?"

Chief Needham coughed into the crook of his arm and then said, "Excuse me. No, ma'am."

The mayor handed a cup to Tanya. "You aren't here for an interrogation."

"We're not?" Sue asked.

The chief of police shook his head. "Your alibi checks out. We spoke with the McGintys this morning, and, according to our other findings, there's no way you could have been responsible for what happened last night."

Ellen heaved a sigh and glanced at her friends. Tanya had tears of relief in her eyes.

"Thank goodness," Sue said.

"What other findings?" Ellen asked.

The mayor took his seat across from Sue, as the chief, who sat at the head of the table, said, "For one thing, there was no homicide. The body you discovered belonged to a man who had been dead for many weeks—dead from a car accident and buried by his family in the city cemetery."

"What?" Sue cried.

"Someone dug up a dead body, carried it to the old hospital site, and mutilated it there," Kiernan explained.

Tanya shivered. "How disgusting. Why would anyone do such a thing?"

"That's the one-million-dollar question," the chief said. "An employee at the cemetery said the grave hadn't been disturbed before he left at 8 p.m. last night. The three witnesses that saw you at the scene of the crime said they followed you to that location from the McGintys. So, you ladies are in the clear."

"If the guy was already dead and buried," Ellen began, "where did the blood come from? I thought people were drained and embalmed before burial."

"A cat," the chief said before he coughed into the crook of his arm. "We found it a few yards away from the body."

Tanya clutched her stomach. "How awful."

"Whose body was it?" Sue asked. "I assume he's been identified?"

"His name was Martin McCready," Chief Needham replied. "He was one of the five hundred people in this town that caught the flu. He died a few weeks ago in a head-on collision."

Ellen chewed on her bottom lip for a moment before asking, "If we're not here for an interrogation, then why are we here?"

"For a *collaboration*," the chief said. "When Kiernan told me why you ladies came to town, I was curious to see if you've discovered anything. The mayor may believe what the doctors are saying about mass hysteria—it's all in our minds—but I *know* how I feel and what I've seen."

"What have you seen?" Sue asked.

"My grandfather," the chief said. "He's been visiting me every night since mid-April. Just before I'm about to go to sleep, he appears at the foot of my bed and looks down at me for twenty, maybe thirty, seconds and then disappears."

"How do you know it's your grandfather?" Ellen asked.

"I recognize him."

"He's a full-bodied apparition?" Sue asked.

"I guess so, though it's not like looking at you and me. He looks sort of like one of those holograms you see in science fiction films, you know what I mean? Like Princess Leia appears in her recording for Obi

Wan, when she says, 'Help me, Obi Wan Kenobi, You're my only hope.'"

Ellen chuckled. "Transparent and luminous?"

"Exactly." The chief laughed.

"Have you tried to talk to him?" Sue asked.

He nodded. "He never talks back. He just appears, stares down at me, no matter what I say or do, and then vanishes."

That sounded to Ellen a lot like what Erin McGinty was experiencing. "Has anyone else seen him?"

"No. I live alone."

Tanya took a sip of her coffee. "Did your grandfather pass recently?"

"It's been years. He was a 31er. Died in December of that year. My father used to tell us stories about what it was like as a child living here while the families tried to scrape by."

Kiernan scratched his chin. "Didn't your father pass about four or five years ago?"

"It'll be five years in November."

"That's what I thought," Kiernan said. "He died of prostate cancer. Isn't that right?"

The chief nodded.

"What about your grandfather?" Tanya asked. "How did he die?"

"Pneumonia. Apparently, it was pretty common back then."

Ellen straightened her back as her mouth fell open.

"Does that mean something to you?" the chief asked Ellen.

Ellen took a pen and notepad from her purse to make a note. "Erin McGinty's great-grandfather died of pneumonia back in the early thirties, and he's been visiting her since mid-April."

"That's interesting." The chief got up and poured himself a cup of coffee. "Very interesting."

"Do you know if he died at the Boulder City Hospital?" Sue asked.

"No. I don't. Why?"

"We have a theory," Ellen explained. "It seems more than coincidental that the flu symptoms and phantom sightings began shortly after the original hospital was torn down."

"That never occurred to me," the chief admitted.

"We should be able to go to the new hospital and ask to see the records," Sue said.

"You'll want to go to the Bureau of Reclamation," Kiernan said. "After Six Companies closed the original hospital in '36, the bureau kept the records."

"I didn't realize it was closed in '36," Tanya said.

"The bureau reopened it in the forties for the treatment of casualties of war," Kiernan explained. "It stayed open until the mid-seventies, when the new hospital was built."

"Does the bureau have an office here in town?" Sue asked.

"Yes, ma'am, about five minutes from here," the chief said.

"That's where we should go next," Sue said. "Don't you ladies agree?"

"Have you spoken with Randy Schams about buying the property?" the mayor asked.

"Not yet. Why?" Ellen asked.

"I think he might be open to working out a good deal," Kiernan said.

Tanya frowned. "I'm not sure we're interested anymore. Are you, guys? I mean, there's something evil on that hill. I don't want anything to do with it."

Ellen sighed. Just last evening, Tanya had been upset by the loss of an important piece of history. She wondered if Tanya would feel differently if she knew what the ghost at the Boulder Dam Hotel had told Sue.

He followed you here.

Not for the first time, Ellen wished they hadn't gone to the old hospital grounds last night.

CHAPTER TEN

The 31ers

Thank you," Ellen said when Chief Needham gave her a list of the over five hundred people who had reported having persistent flu-like symptoms within the last six months. "We'll let you know what we uncover."

"I appreciate that," the chief said as he shook each of their hands. "It was a pleasure to meet you. Here's my card. Let me know if you find anything."

Mayor McManius followed Ellen, Sue, and Tanya from the conference room and out of the Boulder City Police Department, and, as he opened the door to the limo for them, he said, "Oh, I meant to ask if you've had a chance to talk to the 31ers yet."

"We haven't had time," Sue said.

"But it's on the list," Ellen assured him.

"You might want to go now, before you visit the bureau office. All the residents will be in the dining room, waiting for lunch. Otherwise, I'd go around four-thirty, when they're waiting for their dinner."

"That's great advice," Tanya said. "Thanks."

Sue found the card Kiernan had given her the previous evening and read the address to Kirk. Ten minutes later, he pulled the limo in front of Mountain View Nursing Center.

Ellen, Sue, and Tanya were disappointed not to find anyone manning the front desk. After waiting for a few minutes, Ellen decided to look for the dining hall. Sue and Tanya followed.

Around the corner, Ellen found a large, carpeted room with a piano in the back, near a set of French doors flanked by windows overlooking a courtyard. Although the dining hall suffered from that same institutional smell Ellen noticed at most hospital and nursing homes—like a mixture of urine and disinfectant—it looked pleasant enough. About a dozen residents were already seated around the tables, many of them in wheelchairs. Two elderly women were in conversation, but everyone else just sat there, waiting for their lunch, except for one woman, who couldn't seem to stop coughing. Ellen wondered if she was afflicted with the Phantom Flu.

When the residents noticed Ellen and her friends enter the room, many of their faces lit up.

"Hello," one elderly man said from his wheelchair. "It's good to see you."

She returned his smile. "It's good to see you, too. I'm looking for someone. Maybe you can help me?"

"He won't be able to," an elderly woman at another table said. "But I can. Who are you looking for?"

Ellen turned to Sue, who read the three names Kiernan had scribbled onto the back of his card: "Daniel Moore, Joseph Talbot, and Rudy Hicks."

"That's them at the back corner table," she said. "What do you want them for? Are you writing a book about the Hoover Dam?"

"Not exactly," Sue said as they headed over to the furthest end of the room, near the windows.

The three men, one of whom sat in a wheelchair, had been sitting quietly together with dull looks on their faces, but the moment Ellen, Sue, and Tanya approached, they smiled up at them. None of them appeared to be affected by the Phantom Flu.

"Excuse me," Ellen said. "Do you gentlemen mind if we ask you a few questions about what it was like during the days of the building of Hoover Dam?"

"Not at all. Have a seat," the one in the wheelchair said.

Tanya and Ellen pulled chairs from a nearby table. Sue sat in the one beside the man in the wheelchair.

Ellen and her friends introduced themselves.

"I'm Danny Moore," the man in the wheelchair said. The top of his head was bald, and short silver hair grew near his temples. His brows were silver and bushy over very blue eyes. To Ellen, he asked, "Are we related?"

"I don't think so," Ellen said. "My name is spelled differently—M-O-H-R."

"Then you're German," Danny said. "I'm English."

"It's my husband—late husband—who was German," she said, her stomach clenching. "I'm mostly Irish, I think."

"So am I. Joe Talbot. Pleasure to meet you."

Joe had thin wisps of gray hair on his head and, unlike the thin men flanking him, was surprisingly stout for his age.

"And that's Rudy," Danny said. "He just turned one hundred-and-one last week."

"Oldest one here," Rudy, who was bald and had big green eyes, said. "They dug a grave for me a while back, but I've never been very cooperative."

Everyone at the table laughed.

"That might be why you're still alive," Sue teased. "They say only the *good* die young."

The men laughed even louder.

"What can you remember about the original Boulder Dam Hospital?" Ellen asked.

"Nothing," Rudy said. "Only the dam employees were treated there. The wives and kids had to go to the doctors in Vegas."

"Really?" Tanya said. "I wonder why."

"Money," Joe said. "Six Companies couldn't afford healthcare for everyone."

"They could afford it," Rudy said. "They just couldn't make a profit. They only built the hospital because they saw another way to nickel and dime the workers."

"What do you mean?" Sue asked. "Are you saying Six Companies made money from the Boulder Dam Hospital?"

"That's exactly what I'm saying," Rudy said. "They took money out of their workers' paychecks for healthcare, rent, transport, meals, groceries—you name it."

"That seems fair to me," Tanya said.

"Except they always charged more than everything was worth," Rudy said. "Profiteers, that's what they were. The workers had no choice, unless they wanted to go all the way to Vegas."

"My mama used to complain about the meal plan all the time," Joe said. "Six Companies charged $1.50 a day for meals—no other place in sight to get food. My mother worked for the catering firm and knew it only cost them eighty-five cents a day to feed a person."

"Greedy sons of bitches," Rudy said. "Pardon my language, ladies."

"Of course," Ellen said.

"They made money on everything," Danny said. "Nickeled-and-dimed us all."

"The workers only got paid for the time they were on the job," Joe said. "Even though many had no choice but to commute from Las Vegas, which required another three hours per day."

"And if anyone dared to join a labor strike." Danny shook his head.

"Disposable—that's what the workers were—easily replaced by another hungry scab ready to work off his tail for crumbs," Rudy said.

"Didn't Six Companies build the neighborhoods?" Tanya asked.

"And gouged the workers on rent," Rudy said. "They nickeled-and-dimed workers every which way. There were so many deductions that when payday came around, the workers sometimes *owed* money!"

"Was there ever a flu epidemic?" Ellen asked.

"No, but plenty of workers died of pneumonia—or so that's what went on their death certificates," Rudy said.

"What do you mean?" Sue asked. "Did they die of something else?"

"From the gas—carbon monoxide—from being in those tunnels with the trucks running," Joe said.

Ellen's jaw dropped open. "Did you say *gas?*"

Tanya lifted her brows. "That's what James McGinty said."

"We may be onto something," Sue said excitedly.

"James McGinty?" Danny asked. "We knew a James McGinty. I wonder if they're related."

"Why do you think the workers died of carbon monoxide poisoning and not pneumonia?" Ellen asked.

"Six Companies didn't want to have to pay workmen's compensation," Joe said. "They owned the hospital and employed the doctors, so they could strong-arm the doctors into giving a different cause of death."

"How did the workers get carbon monoxide poisoning in the first place?" Sue asked.

"From the tunnels, right?" Tanya asked.

"Right," Rudy said. "See, they had to blast through solid rock to form the diversion tunnels, to divert the river."

"The deeper they went, the worse the ventilation would get," Joe said.

"What are we talking about?" Danny asked Joe suddenly.

"The Hoover Dam," Joe said. "These ladies want to know about the carbon monoxide poisoning."

"Hello, there," Danny said. "You can call me Danny."

"They already know that," Rudy said. Then to Ellen and her friends he said, "Danny resets about every fifteen minutes."

"My apologies," Danny said, red-faced.

"You don't need to apologize," Ellen said. "I forget what I'm doing all the time. I totally understand."

"Me, too," Tanya said.

"I can't tell you how many times I go into the kitchen and forget why I went there," Sue said.

"That happens to all of us," Rudy said.

"I was just telling these ladies that the deeper the dam workers got into the tunnels, the worse the ventilation would be," Joe said.

"That's true," Danny said. "The bulldozer and usually about eighteen dump trucks would fill the tunnels with poisonous carbon monoxide gas while they were being loaded with debris from the dynamite blasts."

"See, it would have been too expensive to bring in a fleet of electrified trucks," Joe explained. "I recall a legal fuss about that, but the feds nipped it in the bud."

"I'll never forget how scared I was when my pa started taking my canaries with him, cage and all," Danny said. "If the birds fainted, the workers knew it was time to get out of there."

"But not every crew happened to have a pair of canaries to warn them," Joe added.

"True," Danny said. "I remember, one night, my pa came home with a hair-raising story. An entire crew was gassed so bad that they had to call Murl Emery out to haul the men upriver to the camp landing, where ambulances carried them to the hospital."

"Boulder City Hospital?" Ellen asked.

"That's right," Danny said. "And guess what they died of."

"Pneumonia?" Sue asked.

"You betcha," Danny said.

"That's why they rushed them to the hospital so fast," Rudy added. "It wasn't to save their lives. Those men were already dying. It was so Six Companies could call it anything but an industrial accident, to get out of paying workmen's comp."

"A man had to die on site to be given workmen's comp," Joe added.

"So those men who were gassed," Ellen began, "they died at Boulder City Hospital?"

"Yep," Danny said.

"One more question," Ellen said, "if you don't mind. How did *your* fathers die? Were they gassed, too?"

"My pops was a high scaler who fell from the canyon wall," Rudy said.

"Oh, how awful," Tanya said. "I'm so sorry."

"My pa was a nipper in Tunnel No. 3, next to the river on the Arizona side. He was run over by a truck," Danny said.

"Run over by a truck?" Sue asked. "How did that happen?"

"While a juicer loaded up the dynamite," Danny began, "the others would move to safety—usually behind and under the trucks. Well, one driver forgot to wait for clearance and ran over my pa."

"Oh my God," Tanya said. "That's so sad."

"I blame Hurry-Up Crowe," Danny said. "My ma did, too. Crowe turned the tunnel blasting into a competition, to see which of the teams could finish the fastest, which made men careless."

"Hurry-Up Crowe?" Ellen asked.

"That was the superintendent," Joe said. "Frank Crowe."

Ellen remembered reading about him at the Boulder Dam Hotel Museum.

"And what about *your* father?" Sue asked Joe.

"He was a mucker killed by a surprise delayed explosion."

"That's horrible," Tanya said. "I wonder if people would have taken such dangerous jobs during any other time in American history—I mean regular civilians, of course."

"I think we have what we need," Ellen said to Sue and Tanya. "Why don't we go to the bureau office from here?"

"Thank you, gentlemen," Tanya said.

"Yes," Sue said. "Thanks so much for your time."

"It was a pleasure," Rudy said.

"Goodbye," Ellen said.

Ten minutes later, Kirk dropped Ellen, Sue, and Tanya in front of the Bureau of Reclamation Office, a white L-shaped one-story building with a red-tiled roof. As Ellen and her friends walked along the sidewalk past a flagpole to a door with no signage, Ellen wondered if they were in the right place.

"Is this the front entrance?" Tanya wondered.

"Only one way to find out." Sue opened the door and led the way inside.

They walked on rickety floorboards toward a window, with a woman sitting at a desk on the other side, reminding Ellen of her doctor's office.

"Can I help you?" the woman asked.

Ellen approached the window. "Would it be possible for us to look at Hoover Dam fatality records and death certificates from the Boulder City Hospital from 1931 to 1935?"

"You'll want to inquire at our Records Office, which is down the hall, second room on the left."

"Thank you," Ellen said.

The Records Office resembled a library, with six rows of books on the right and a front desk on the left. In between the stacks and the desk was a long conference-style table with a dozen wooden chairs around it.

On the desk was a bell with a sign that read, "Ring for service." Since there was nobody in sight, Sue rang the bell.

"Can I help you?" A woman emerged from one of the rows of books. She had short red hair, round glasses, and a tall, thin figure, like Tanya.

"We're looking for Hoover Dam fatality records," Ellen said, "and hospital records of death certificates issued between 1931 to 1935. Can you help us?"

"I certainly can. Are you writing a book?"

"Not exactly," Sue said.

"We're collaborating with Chief Needham," Tanya said. "Looking for answers that might explain what's going on in Boulder City."

"Oh, I see," she said, rolling her eyes. "More ghost hunters."

"Have you been visited by many paranormal investigators?" Sue asked.

"A few," she said. "But no one's asked to see the hospital records. I'll be right back, if you'd like to have a seat." She motioned to the conference table.

Sue sat at one end of the table as Ellen and Tanya sat at her left and right.

Tanya whispered, "I don't like the way she rolled her eyes."

"Me either," Sue said.

Ellen said nothing, because it wasn't that long ago when she would have rolled her eyes, too.

A few minutes later, the woman returned with two folders—one thin and the other thick. The woman said that they would find a list of all the Hoover Dam related deaths in the thin folder and all the death certificates issued by the hospital in the 1930's in the second folder.

"Thank you," Ellen said.

Sue opened the thin folder. On the first page was a chart with columns for date, name, cause of death, and employer. The dates ranged from May to December of 1931, but the entries weren't in chronological order; rather, they were organized by cause of death, the first being heat prostration.

"Sixteen people, including two women, died of heat prostration," Tanya pointed out.

"Two men drowned," Sue said, "though there's a side note that two others drowned—one in 1921 and another in 1922."

"Seven men died from blasting," Ellen read. "And six more from falling rock or slides."

"Other industrial accidents took three men," Tanya read. "It looks like Danny's father wasn't the only one who was run over by a truck."

"Eleven more people died of natural causes," Sue said.

"Only six of those were pneumonia," Ellen pointed out. "That's not very convincing evidence."

"But look at the names," Sue said. "Wolff, Cliff, Needham, Minton, Dorr, McCarthy."

"Chief Needham," Tanya said.

"Do we have anyone on the list with the other last names?" Ellen pulled the list from her purse and unfolded it. "We do: seven Cliffs, ten Dorrs…let's see, fifteen McCarthys, seven Mintons, twelve Needhams, and, let's see, three Wolffs."

Sue laid the first page down, so they could study the second, which had a similar chart with dates from 1932.

Ellen scanned down the list to the bottom, where *Natural Causes* were listed. "Oh my gosh! Fifteen men died of pneumonia, and many of those were within days of one another."

"Look at these names." Sue put her finger beneath two names.

"McGinty and McCready," Tanya read. "James McGinty—Erin's great grandfather."

"And McCready was the name of the man whose body we found mutilated at the old hospital grounds," Sue said.

Ellen's heart picked up speed. "I think we're on the right track."

On the third page, they found eight more deaths from pneumonia from 1933, all within a few days of one another. The names on the list matched names of current people in Boulder City suffering from the Phantom Flu. Nine more deaths from pneumonia were reported in 1934 and two more in 1935; however, when Ellen looked more carefully, she noticed more deaths during both years listed as Septecemia Pneuomcoccic and Bronchopneumonia.

"Look at this," Ellen said, pointing at statistics listed on the bottom of the fifth page. "This page reports forty-two deaths by pneumonia during the building of the dam. Pneumonia killed more men than any other cause of death, and that number doesn't include the men who died from Septecemia Pneuomcoccic and Bronchopneumonia."

"We need to see if pneumonia was as widespread among family members," Tanya said. "If pneumonia was as common among non-workers as it was among workers, then we won't have a case."

"Before we go, let's see how many of these men died at Boulder City Hospital," Ellen said, opening the thicker folder.

Ellen and her friends spent an hour matching forty-eight names from the fatality records to death certificates showing the place of death at Boulder City Hospital, leaving less than ten deaths from pneumonia occurring at home from 1931 to 1935.

When they asked the office worker to point them in the direction of a copy machine, the woman said, "I can make those copies for you."

"Oh, thank you!" Ellen said.

"I'm glad you found what you were looking for," the woman said.

"We still need to compare these statistics to records from the hospital in Las Vegas during the same time period," Tanya said.

"We have those records here, too," the woman said.

Ellen and her friends lifted their brows and smiled.

"Really?" Ellen asked. "Why would you have the Las Vegas Hospital records?"

"Clark County Hospital opened in Vegas in 1931 and in 1943 was turned over to the federal government. That's when we took possession of the records."

"Lucky for us," Sue said. "Can we see death certificates from 1931 to 1935?"

"I'll grab those for you," the woman said. "Then you can tell me which records you'd like copies of."

"Thank you," Tanya said.

A few minutes later, the woman returned with another thick folder with death certificates from the 1930s from Clark County Hospital. Ellen, Sue, and Tanya poured over the documents for another hour and found only ten deaths due to pneumonia over all five years in which the Hoover Dam was built.

"This has got to be the problem," Ellen said. "The ghosts of workers who were unjustly diagnosed and denied workmen's compensation were stuck at the Boulder City Hospital. Then, when Schams and his company tore it down, the ghosts were released all over the city."

"It makes sense that the ghosts would search for their descendants," Tanya said.

Sue cocked her head to the side. "But why give them the Phantom Flu?"

Tanya shrugged. "If I were a ghost, I wouldn't make my own descendants suffer."

"Maybe they didn't," Ellen said. "Maybe the evil thing you sensed at the old hospital grounds gave them the flu."

"That makes more sense," Tanya said. "But what is that evil thing? A demon?"

"Maybe it's the ghost of Frank Crowe or someone from Six Companies," Sue said.

"The message in blood said, 'I did as I was told,'" Ellen reminded them.

Tanya's eyes widened. "It's a doctor!"

"Do you think the spirit of a doctor turned evil?" Sue asked.

"Maybe," Ellen said. "Maybe he's tormented by what he did."

"Let's check out the names of the doctors on the death certificates." Sue opened the first thick folder containing records from Boulder City Hospital.

"Dr. Anthony Bridgewater," Tanya read as she combed through one record after another. "Bridgewater. Bridgewater. Oh, my God. He's listed on every single one of the death certificates listing pneumonia as the cause of death!"

"This is exciting!" Sue said. "A break in the case!"

"I think so, too!" Ellen said.

"We deserve a delicious lunch," Sue said. "I saw a café on the way with a sign that said *Homemade Cheesecake*."

"Sounds good," Tanya said. "Let's get our copies and go!"

CHAPTER ELEVEN

A City Council Meeting

With a Mediterranean vibe, Milo's Inn and Café offered a spectacular menu. Ellen ordered La Parisian—turkey, brie, cucumber, tomato, greens, and dijonnaise on a homemade croissant—with a cup of French onion soup. Tanya ordered the Greek wrap—kalamata olives, pepperoncinis, feta cheese, spring mix, romaine, cucumber, and tomato with red wine vinaigrette. And Sue ordered the lobster and crab roll—Lobster meat and herbed mayo with lemon served on a toasted homemade roll. Since it wasn't too hot outside, they sat on a shaded patio beneath a vine-covered arbor among Greek statues and the calming trickle of water from a nearby fountain. While they waited for their food to arrive, they sipped iced tea and snacked on warm pita dipped in delicious hummus.

Sue fished something from her purse and brought out Kiernan's card. "I'm going to text the mayor and let him know what we discovered."

"I'll text Brian," Ellen said.

"Someone should tell the chief," Tanya pointed out.

"Oh," Ellen said, digging into her purse. "I have his card. Here you go Tanya."

"I don't want to call him," she said. "You call him."

When Ellen finished texting Brian, she called Chief Needham and relayed their theory to him.

"There's a special city council meeting going on right now," the chief said. "I believe it runs until four o'clock. I don't suppose you'd meet me there to share your findings?"

"We just ordered lunch," Ellen said. "It might take a while."

"Take your time," he said. "Could you meet me there around 3:30?"

"Hold on a second," she said. Then, turning to her friends, she asked, "Should we present our findings to the city council today, around 3:30?"

"Kiernan just texted me that same question," Sue said.

"We should go," Tanya said. "We can make it by then, don't you think?"

Ellen told the chief they'd be there. Sue texted Kiernan the same.

After lunch, Ellen and her friends asked Kirk to drive them to City Hall, which was only a block or so away from their hotel. They walked past a flagpole and a sculpture of playing children before climbing a few steps to the glass front doors. A sign pointed them in the direction of the city council chambers, where they found the meeting already in progress. They were met at the door by Chief Needham, who led them to three empty chairs in the back row. Ten rows of chairs were split down the middle, at the end of which was a podium, where a tall, older woman, perhaps in her mid-seventies, was addressing the council.

The council members were seated around a semicircular desk on a dais, facing the audience. Kiernan sat in the middle and was flanked by three other members on either side, to total seven council members. On one end of the semicircular desk, a man hunched over a tripod with a video recorder perched on it. On the other end, another man seemed to be taking notes on a laptop computer.

"I know we're all distracted by this flu crisis," the woman at the podium was saying into the microphone. "But we can't neglect the application for the Nevada Historic Preservation Fund. Is anybody working on that? If not, I volunteer."

"Councilwoman Andrea Miller," the mayor said, "can you address the speaker regarding that application?"

"Yes, I can," one of the council members said. "The application was sent three days ago."

"Thank you," the woman at the podium said before taking her seat.

Next, a young man approached the podium and asked about the energy assistance program. Another council member answered the question.

Ellen's back straightened when a young woman approached the podium and, after coughing for a few seconds, introduced herself as Haley Cliff—a surname which Ellen recognized was among those listed as having died in 1931 of pneumonia.

"Has the council taken any more measures to help those of us who are suffering with this flu? Has any progress been made? My children and I are exhausted from all this coughing."

"As a matter of fact," Kiernan said, "some interesting information has just been brought to light by three guests who have been collaborating with Chief Needham. Chief? Would you please bring Ellen Mohr, Sue Graham, and Tanya Sanchez to the podium?"

As Haley Cliff returned to her seat, Chief Needham offered a hand to Sue, who was seated on the aisle, and led her up to the podium. Ellen and Tanya followed. Ellen knew Tanya wouldn't want to speak, but she wasn't sure whether Sue wanted to. When Sue made no move for the microphone, Ellen supposed she would be the one to address the council.

"Thank you, Chief Needham and Mayor McManius," Ellen said. "And thanks to the rest of the council for allowing me to present our recent findings. My friends and I comprise a paranormal investigation team…" Ellen paused when more than a few groans swept through the room.

"Please be civil toward our guests, people," Kiernan said. "Let's hear what they have to say."

"Thank you, Mayor McManius," Ellen said. "My team and I investigated at the home of Mary Jane McGinty, whose daughter Erin suffers from the Phantom Flu and has experienced ghost sightings since mid-April. During our investigation, we, along with Erin, Mary Jane, and one other person, witnessed an apparition. We attempted to make contact with the spirit using an Ouija Board."

Several people in the room gasped.

"After asking the ghost to tell us his name, the planchette spelled out *James*," Ellen said. "Mary Jane said that was the name of her husband's grandfather, so we asked the spirit if his name was James McGinty, and the planchette moved to *YES*."

Someone in the audience said, "This is a waste of time."

"Please refrain from making any derogatory comments," Kiernan said. "Please continue, Mrs. Mohr."

Ellen swallowed hard, trying to remain calm, though she was angry at the reception she was receiving in a town she was trying to help. "After asking the spirit, whom we believed to be James McGinty, if he had a message for us, the planchette spelled the word *gas*."

Sue nudged Ellen to the side and leaned toward the microphone. "We should first explain that we believe it's more than a coincidence that some of you started seeing ghosts shortly after the original Boulder City Hospital was torn down."

The people in the audience seemed to respond more positively to Sue's comment, so she continued, "The hospital was torn down in February, and the first case of the Phantom Flu occurred in March. Both Erin McGinty and Chief Needham have been seeing ancestors who died during the building of the Hoover Dam since mid-April. An interesting connection between Erin McGinty and Chief Needham is that both of their ancestors have death certificates citing pneumonia as the cause of death."

"And both ancestors died at the original Boulder City Hospital," Ellen added.

"That's right," Sue said.

"Today," Ellen continued, "we visited the Bureau of Reclamation Office and found that all five hundred plus victims of the Phantom Flu are descendants of men whose death certificates indicate pneumonia as the cause of death and Boulder City Hospital as the place of death."

"That's incredible," one of the council members muttered into her microphone as people in the audience also reacted, speaking among themselves. "Did you bring copies of this evidence, by any chance?"

"We have it out in the limo," Sue said. "Tanya, can you text Kirk to bring the documents inside?"

Tanya pulled out her phone and began texting.

"Quiet down, please," Mayor Kiernan said to the audience.

"We discovered something else," Ellen said into the microphone. "From 1931 to 1935, over forty deaths were ascribed to pneumonia, the cause of the greatest number of deaths to dam workers. Yet, when we looked at death certificates from Clark County General in Las Vegas, where the families of dam workers were treated, we found only ten pneumonia-related deaths reported over the same number of years. That's a huge discrepancy."

"Couldn't that discrepancy be explained by the fact that dam workers were in close quarters, where viruses and bacteria can more easily be passed from person to person?" a councilman asked.

"Weren't the workers and their families living in close quarters?" Sue replied. "From what I understand, they weren't living in mansions."

A few people chuckled.

"Mention the doctor," Tanya whispered to Sue and Ellen.

"And one more interesting fact worth mentioning," Ellen said. "The same doctor at Boulder City Hospital signed all forty-eight death certificates citing pneumonia as the cause of death—a doctor who was employed by Six Companies."

"Are you suggesting that Six Companies coerced a doctor into making a fraudulent diagnosis on those death certificates?" the mayor asked.

"*We* aren't," Sue said. "The 31ers we spoke to at Mountain View suggested it. Joe Talbot, Rudy Hicks, and Danny Moore believe that Six Companies didn't want to pay workmen's compensation to workers who were gassed in the tunnels by carbon monoxide."

Ellen leaned toward the microphone. "The 31ers also said that Six Companies went to extreme measures to get gas victims off the dam site and to Boulder City Hospital before they died."

Kirk entered and met Tanya, who passed the copies from the bureau to Chief Needham. The Chief looked over the documents before handing them to the mayor.

As the mayor looked over the records, Ellen said, "I believe that the ghosts that some of you have been seeing might be able to pass on and find peace if these records were amended. Maybe a note could be made that we now suspect that these men died of carbon monoxide poisoning. That simple acknowledgment might be enough."

Sue added, "And if that doesn't work, you might think about giving reparations to the descendants of these workers, who should have received workmen's compensation. Even a small token might be enough to make the spirits feel at peace."

"Do you believe this will also eradicate the flu-like symptoms plaguing their descendants?" the mayor asked.

Ellen, Sue, and Tanya looked at one another.

"We're not sure," Ellen said. "We have another theory about that."

"Would you mind sharing it with the rest of us?" Kiernan asked.

Ellen, not wanting to cause more negative reactions in the audience, encouraged Sue, who was the bravest of the three, to answer. Sue leaned over the podium and, speaking into the microphone, said, "We would rather wait to disclose that theory once we have evidence to back it up."

The believers in the crowd complained while the skeptics balked and rolled their eyes.

"Thank you, ladies," Kiernan said. "The council will consider your recommendations regarding the official death records."

Ellen and Chief Needham followed Sue and Tanya from the city council chambers, down the hall, and outside the building, where the chief thanked them for their help.

"I truly believe you ladies might be onto something," he said. "And I'm wondering if you'd share your other theory regarding the Phantom Flu with me."

Sue glanced at Ellen, who nodded. Then Sue said, "We think the doctor who signed all those death certificates has been tortured by guilt for nearly a century and may have transformed into something evil."

"You think this evil spirit is responsible for the flu?" he asked.

Ellen and her friends nodded. "We aren't sure how or why—and by that, I mean what the doctor would gain from it—but we'll continue to investigate and hopefully find more answers."

"Let me know if I can help in any way," the chief said.

"Do you think the council will amend the records?" Tanya asked.

"I hope so," he said. "If for no other reason than to test your theory. As much as I loved my grandfather, I'd rather his ghost not visit me every night."

"We understand," Tanya said. "Believe me."

They said goodbye to the chief and, as Ellen followed Sue and Tanya into the back of the limo, she thought she heard someone whisper, "Coward." But when she glanced behind her, there was no one there.

CHAPTER TWELVE

Paranormal Evidence

Later that evening, after dinner, Kirk helped Ellen, Sue, and Tanya to lug their equipment from the trunk of the limo into Sue's hotel suite, where they could review and analyze their recordings. The suite consisted of a bedroom, bathroom, and sitting room with a couch, rocking chair, and flat-screen television. Ellen and Sue sat on opposite ends of the couch, while Tanya worked in a rocking chair in the corner of the room, near the window. Each held one of the three full-spectrum cameras and was reviewing the footage. They wore headphones, to increase their chances of picking up on sounds they might not have heard during the investigation.

As Ellen watched and listened to the events that had transpired during their investigation, she became alarmed by the appearance of an orb near Erin's head. The orb appeared early in the investigation, just as Ellen had pressed play on her audio recorder and had called out to the spirits.

What was alarming about the orb was that it almost seemed to come from Erin's head. Just as Tanya had whispered, "The temperature has dropped to seventy degrees—make that sixty-nine," the orb flew from Erin's head to the front door, just before Brian turned toward the door and said, "What was that?"

From there, the orb moved to the front window, behind Mary Jane, after which Mary Jane said, "I felt something, too."

Seconds later, the orb transformed into a nearly full-bodied, albeit transparent, apparition of a man, after which Erin begged it to leave her alone.

As Mary Jane moved beside her daughter, Ellen heard something coming through her speakers. She stopped the camera and played it back, noticing that Sue and Tanya seemed to be doing the same thing.

Ellen lifted her headphones. "Did you hear something?"

"Did you see the orb?" Tanya asked.

"Yes!" Sue said. "Yes, to both."

"Was that James McGinty, do you think?" Tanya asked. "Was he attached to Erin?"

"That's what it looked like," Ellen said. "Do you think that's what's causing the flu? Could the ghosts be attaching themselves to their descendants and feeding off them?"

"There are more descendants than ghosts," Sue pointed out. "Wouldn't there only be forty-eight or so people with the flu?"

"Not if they detach and reattach to other descendants," Tanya said.

"Why don't we try to figure out that sound we just heard," Ellen suggested. "Then we can look for any correlation between Erin's symptoms and the proximity of the apparition to her body."

Ellen replayed the footage, listening very carefully. She replayed it again, with the volume turned up. When she slowed down the audio, she heard a deep voice say something like, *Um losss.*

"I think I hear *I'm lost*," Sue said.

Ellen played it back again. *Um lossst.*

This time she caught the "t" sound at the end. "I think you're right, Sue! He's saying he's lost, just as he said on the Ouija Board."

Ellen continued to review the feed, listening closely to herself say, "Who are you? What's your name?"

Ellen heard another low, guttural sound. At first, it sounded like, *Trey Tee*, but when she played it back, a little more slowly, she heard, *James McGinty*, clear as day.

She stopped the recording and pulled off her headphones, just as her friends were doing the same.

"He said his name!" Sue cried

"I'm so glad we captured this, guys!" Tanya said. "No one ever has much faith in the evidence we get from the Ouija Board, but this is indisputable."

Ellen sighed. "There will always be a skeptic somewhere that will say we messed with the recording."

"True," Tanya admitted.

They returned their headphones to their heads and continued to review their coverage.

Ellen watched herself on camera asking, "Why are you here?"

Again, she heard, *Um Losss*.

And after she asked, "Do you have a message for us?", she heard *Assss*.

She had a hunch he was saying, "Gas," since that's what he'd spelled on the Ouija Board. To be sure, she stopped the recording and played it back more slowly. Sure enough, she was able to detect the hard "g."

Sue had already taken off her headphones. Ellen and Tanya did the same.

Sue said, "Did you hear him say, 'I'm lost' again?"

"Yes!" Ellen said.

"And after you ask if he has a message for us, he says, 'Gas,'" Tanya said. "Did you get that, too?"

Sue and Ellen nodded excitedly.

"Did you see what he did with his face and hands while he said it?" Sue asked.

"No," Ellen said. She returned her headphones to her head and rewound the tape, watching the apparition carefully when she came to the part where he said, "Gas."

She saw him make a motion with his hands in front of his face. He touched the tips of the fingers on each hand to one another and then quickly opened his hands and arms, as if demonstrating an explosion, after which, he hung his head to the side.

Ellen paused the recording and said, "He was indicating the dynamite exploding. He wants us to know he was hurt in the diversion tunnels."

"It's not super-obvious," Tanya said, "but that's what I got out of it, too."

Ellen continued the recording, watching the part with the Ouija Board.

When Erin asked, "Why are you haunting me? How could you do this to me, if you're my great-grandfather?"

Ellen heard, *Um loss* again as the planchette spelled I-M-L-O-S-T.

As soon as Erin said that she heard something outside, the transparent and luminous apparition became an orb, about the size of an orange, and returned to the back of Erin's head, where it disappeared.

Ellen stopped the recording and pulled off the headphones. "I think he's attached to Erin."

"Let's watch the rest of the footage," Sue said.

Ellen returned the headphones to her head and pressed play. She saw nothing unusual until Tanya, in the recording, asked, "Did he die tragically? Was he killed on the job?" and Mary Jane replied, "No, not at all. Fred told me that his father died of pneumonia."

At that moment, the orb rushed from Erin's head and ran into the floor lamp, causing the bulb to flicker and the lamp to move. They hadn't noticed the lamp move, because they'd been too startled by the flickering light. The orb flew around the room before it seemed to reenter Erin's head.

Nothing else unusual occurred during the remainder of the coverage.

When the recording ended, Ellen took off the headphones for the last time and said, "If he's attached to her, a circle of protection won't help her."

"We need to perform a crossover ceremony," Sue said.

Tanya nodded. "As soon as possible."

When Ellen, Sue, and Tanya arrived at the McGinty house twenty minutes later, it was almost eleven o'clock. Dead-dog-tired and armed with nothing more than their *gris gris* bags, sage smudge stick, and Sue's holy water, the three friends got to work bathing themselves and the two McGintys in smoke from the burning sage. Erin broke into coughing fits, alarming Mary Jane, but Ellen and her friends explained that the smoke was a necessary protection.

Ellen set up one of the three spectrum cameras, while Sue created a circle of protection with a line of salt around the perimeter of the room, to prevent other spirits from harming them as they conducted the crossover ceremony. Ellen noticed that the line of salt from the day before hadn't been vacuumed.

Tanya put the Ouija Board on the coffee table, along with a temperature gauge and an EMF detector. Once they had everything set up, they took a few readings before turning off the lamp to begin.

Ellen, Sue, and Tanya took their seats on the couches around the coffee table as Erin sat in her recliner and her mother stood beside her, holding her hand.

Ellen took a deep breath and said, "We're here to speak with James McGinty, who died of carbon monoxide poisoning. It happened during the building of the Hoover Dam. James McGinty, we're here to help you find your way. We understand that you're lost and that your spirit couldn't move on because of the injustice done to you by Six Companies and Dr. Bridgewater. We want you to move on and find peace. If you can hear us, please give us a sign."

Suddenly Tanya flinched.

"What happened?" Sue, beside her, asked.

"The planchette moved. Did anyone else see that?" Tanya glanced at Erin and Mary Jane, who shook their heads. "I know I didn't imagine that."

"Maybe he wants us to use the Ouija Board," Ellen said. "Should we?"

The three friends placed their fingertips on the planchette.

"James McGinty?" Sue said. "Are you here with us?"

The planchette moved to YES.

"Are you ready to move on and find peace?" Ellen asked.

The planchette moved to NO.

Tanya's brows furrowed. "I wonder why?"

The planchette began to move again. It stopped on S before moving to O-M-E-O-N-E-E-L-S-E-I-S-H-E-R-E."

"Someone else is here?" Sue repeated. "Someone besides the five of us and you?"

The planchette moved to YES.

A shiver worked down Ellen's spine.

"He doesn't want to leave because someone else is here," Tanya whispered. "Do you think this other entity is holding him back?"

"Who?" Erin asked. "Who else is here?"

The planchette spelled B-A-D-I-D-O-N-T-K-N-O-W.

"Someone bad, that he doesn't know," Tanya whispered.

"Who?" Mary Jane said as tears filled her eyes. "Is it because I let them use the Ouija Board? Did I allow a demon into my house? Oh, my Jesus, please protect us from the evils of hell!"

Erin screamed and pulled the quilt over her head. Mary Jane wrapped her arms around her daughter.

Ellen began to fear that she and her friends weren't prepared for whatever it was they had gotten themselves into. "Maybe we should try to speak to the other presence."

"I think Erin and I should go and stay with my sister-in-law," Mary Jane said.

"Don't break the circle of protection," Tanya said. "Wait until we know it's safe."

"It may never be safe!" Erin said as she cried into her quilt.

"Please give us a little more time," Sue said.

"I'll wait a few more minutes," Mary Jane said, "and then I'm taking my baby girl away from here."

"You have no way of knowing whether it will follow you," Ellen said, wondering if it was possible that the evil thing from the old hospital grounds had followed them to the hotel *and* to the McGinty residence.

Sue met her gaze. She seemed to be thinking the same thing.

"Oh, spirits of the other realm," Ellen said. "We come in peace. We mean you no harm. If you are here, and if your name is not James McGinty, would you please give us a sign?"

Ellen was startled by a loud knock just above her head.

"Have you ever heard that noise before?" Sue asked Mary Jane.

Mrs. McGinty shook her head.

"Is there an attic above us?" Tanya asked.

"Yes," Mary Jane said. "I keep my Christmas decorations up there."

"Have you ever had rats or other pests up there?" Ellen asked.

"Not that I'm aware of," Mary Jane said.

"What about those other ghost hunters?" Tanya asked. "Have they come around since last night?"

Mary Jane shook her head.

"Spirits of the other realm," Sue said. "If you are not James McGinty, please knock again."

The knock, from above, came again, as loudly as before.

"If you are not James McGinty," Sue asked, "are you someone else who was alive during the building of the Hoover Dam? Please knock once for yes or twice for no."

Another knock.

"Did you also die of carbon monoxide poisoning?" Sue asked. "Please knock once for yes, or twice for no."

Two knocks.

"No," Tanya whispered.

"Did you work for Six Companies?" Sue asked.

One knock.

"Yes," Tanya whispered.

"Ask him if he's bad," Erin said from beneath her quilt.

Before Sue could reply, they heard two knocks.

"He's not bad." Erin lifted her head from the quilt.

"Or he's lying," Sue said. "Why don't you let me ask the questions from now on, okay, Erin?"

Erin nodded.

"Spirit, if you are not James McGinty," Sue began, "will you spell your name by moving this planchette on the board? Knock once for yes, or twice for no."

Two knocks.

"It doesn't want us to know its name," Tanya whispered.

"Are you Dr. Bridgewater?" Ellen asked.

Two knocks.

"No," Tanya whispered.

Ellen wondered if the spirit was lying.

"Do you have a message for us?" Sue asked.

One knock.

"Will you spell out your message using this planchette on the board?" Sue asked.

One knock.

Ellen watched as the planchette began to move beneath her fingertips. Quickly, its spelled G-O-H-O-M-E.

"Go home," Tanya whispered.

"Do you want us to return to our hotel?" Sue asked.

Two knocks.

Suddenly the planchette spelled L-E-A-V-E-T-O-W-N.

"Why?" Sue asked.

Mortal terror consumed Ellen as multiple knocks sounded above them, as if someone were throwing a ball around in the attic. The knocks came from different spots on the ceiling. Ellen wasn't sure what to do.

Whether it was fear or bravery, Ellen climbed to her feet, balled her fists, and shouted, "I know who you are, Dr. Anthony Bridgewater! I'm onto you! I know what you did, and so will the rest of the world!"

The knocks stopped, and, except for Erin's sobs, the room was filled with silence.

Sue and Tanya, whose fingertips continued to rest on the planchette, gasped as the plastic indicator moved to NO. Then it spelled K-A-H-N.

"What does that mean?" Tanya whispered.

"Is that your name?" Sue asked. "Is your name Kahn?"

One knock.

"His name is Kahn, and he worked for Six Companies," Tanya whispered.

Sue took out her phone and, after tapping on it, read, "Ferris Kahn of MacDonald and Kahn Company served as the Treasurer for Six Companies during the construction of the Hoover Dam."

Suddenly, the knocks above came fast and hard, like hail. Mary Jane turned on the floor lamp, but the bulb flickered and went out.

"Don't break the circle!" Tanya shouted, because Mary Jane had moved toward a light switch.

As the knocks pounded harder and faster, Erin covered her ears and screamed. Sue stood up and took a vial of holy water from her purse before flinging the water into the air and letting it fall on the furniture, people, and carpeting.

Sue cried, "I rebuke you in the name of Abraham! In the name of Moses! In the name of Elijah! I rebuke you in the name of Jesus! In the name of Mohammed! In the name of God, the Father almighty! I rebuke you evil spirit! Fly away, never to return!"

The knocking ceased.

Everyone was silent for a full minute until Erin began to cough.

"Do you think it's gone?" Mary Jane asked Ellen and her friends.

"For now," Sue said.

"But James McGinty may still be with us," Tanya whispered.

Aloud, Ellen asked, "James? Are you still here?"

Of its own accord, the planchette moved across the board to YES.

Everyone stared at the Ouija Board. Ellen held her breath.

"Listen to me," Tanya said to Erin. "We need to help your great-grandfather to crossover, or you won't ever feel better, okay?"

Erin nodded.

"You need to tell him to leave your body and to look for the light on the other side," Tanya told her. "I think he thinks he's protecting you."

"What if he is?" Mary Jane asked.

"An attached spirit can be just as dangerous as anything evil," Tanya said. "It sucks up your life force. You have to tell it to leave your body!"

Erin's eyes widened as her face turned white. Trembling, she shouted, "Great-granddad, James McGinty, if you care about your own descendant, leave my body!"

"Look for the light and cross to the other side!" Sue added. "Find your peace!"

"Please, great-granddad!" Erin cried as her body was wracked by sobs.

Erin cried and coughed into her quilt as her mother stroked her hair.

Then the floor lamp suddenly turned back on, and Erin flinched, as if she'd touched a hot stove.

"Are you okay, sweetie?" her mother asked.

Erin glanced at everyone in the room. "I think so. I'm not sure."

"What happened just then, when you flinched?" her mother asked.

Erin took a drink from the water bottle on the end table near the recliner. "I don't know. I feel different, though."

"Different? How?" Ellen asked.

"I-I think he left. I think he's gone."

"But how do you *feel?*" Tanya asked her.

"Still tired, but better. I don't feel like I have crud in my throat and lungs. I can breathe."

Mary Jane burst into tears and fell on her knees, pressing her face into her daughter's lap as she sobbed.

"Oh, Mama, it's okay."

Tears fell down Ellen's cheeks, too, as she watched the relief that filled Mary Jane's entire body. Her body shuddered out all the fear and despair that had possessed her for months. Erin may have been possessed by a spirit, but Mary Jane had suffered, too.

CHAPTER THIRTEEN

More Ghosts

That night, Ellen slept between Tanya and Sue in Sue's king-sized bed surrounded by a circle of protection. They had put cups of water at the cardinal points and had closed it with an incantation, just to be extra safe. Ellen was so tired, that even Sue's snoring couldn't keep her from falling asleep. But in the middle of the night, they were awakened by the sound of running water.

"Do you hear that?" Ellen asked Tanya, who had sat up in bed.

"Is Sue taking a shower?"

"No," Sue said. "I'm right here."

Sue turned on the bedside lamp. "Why would I be taking a shower in the middle of the night?"

"To help you fall asleep?" Tanya said sleepily. "I don't know."

The running water sounded like it was coming from the bathroom.

"What time is it?" Ellen asked.

"A few minutes after three," Sue said.

"Should we check the bathroom?" Ellen asked.

"I don't think we should break the circle of protection," Tanya said. "If it's a plumbing problem, it can wait until morning."

Ellen reached over Sue to grab her phone, which was charging on the bedside table. She was surprised to find texts from both Mary Jane McGinty and Chief Needham.

"Listen to this text from Mary Jane: 'My sister-in-law called tonight to say that she and her two boys are fully recovered from the flu. Whatever you did helped them, too. I can't thank you enough!'"

Sue sat up, her tired eyes drooping with bags. "Another break in the case!"

"So, it's for sure not the doctor causing the Phantom Flu," Ellen surmised.

Tanya covered her mouth. "The ancestors must be attaching to their descendants and causing the symptoms."

"But why?" Ellen said. "Maybe to get the energy they need to give us their message?"

"Does this mean we have to help forty-seven more spirits to find peace?" Sue wondered. "That's a lot of crossover ceremonies."

"Maybe there's a way to do them all at once," Tanya said. "Could we do the ceremony at the cemetery, do you think?"

"That's not a bad idea," Ellen said. "I wonder where the bodies are buried."

"I'll look it up in the morning," Sue said as she laid back down to go to sleep. "I wish we had a Voodoo Doughnut here."

"Before you doze off," Ellen said, "listen to this text from Chief Needham: 'Wanted to let you know that we found the culprit responsible for what you found on the old hospital estate last night. Call me in the morning.'"

"Is he referring to an actual person or a ghost?" Tanya said as she stifled a yawn.

"I guess we'll find out in the morning," Ellen said.

"Wait a minute," Sue said. "Be quiet for a minute and listen."

Everyone stayed still and said nothing for over fifteen seconds. Ellen held her breath.

"I don't hear anything," Ellen finally said.

"That's what I'm saying," Sue said. "The water stopped running."

"Now I'm super curious to go and look in the bathroom," Ellen said.

Tanya grabbed her arm. "Don't do it. Maybe it's taunting us, to get us to leave the circle."

Ellen felt bad that she and Sue hadn't told Tanya about the lobby ghost's warning. "Sue, we should tell Tanya."

"Tell me what?"

Sue groaned and rolled over, nestling her face in her pillow.

Ellen told Tanya what happened to Sue in the lobby the previous night.

"What do you think that means?" Tanya asked. "*He followed you here.*"

The water in the bathroom started running again, and all three women jumped.

"Geez Louise," Ellen whispered.

"Tell me what you think it means," Tanya repeated.

Sue closed her eyes and tried to go back to sleep.

Ellen sighed. "We thought the lobby ghost might be referring to the evil shadow man that Brian saw on the old hospital grounds."

Tanya shuddered. "Shit. I hope not. I can't believe you're just now telling me this."

"If the chief has found the person responsible," Ellen began, "then doesn't that mean there wasn't an evil shadow man?"

"No!" Tanya crossed her arms. "The shadow man may have taken possession of the poor human being who's now being blamed for what the demon made him do!"

The water now sounded as if it had been turned on full blast.

Ellen scooted to the end of the bed. "This has gone on long enough."

"Don't break the circle!" Sue and Tanya shouted at the same time.

Ellen stopped just short of the line of salt and then sank back down on the bed. "Fine. But how are we going to get any sleep?"

The sound of snoring coming from Sue's side of the bed made Ellen and Tanya giggle.

"At least one of us can sleep," Tanya whispered.

Ellen was relieved to see morning light filtering into the hotel room from the tops of the curtains, because this meant it was morning, when spirits tended to have less power.

Sue continued to snore beside her, but Tanya startled Ellen by saying, "Good morning."

"Did you get any sleep?" Ellen asked her.

"A little. I've been awake for a while, and I really have to pee, but I'm afraid to go alone."

"I don't hear the water running anymore," Ellen said.

"It wasn't running when I woke up."

"Should we go and check it out?" Ellen asked.

Tanya nodded.

Ellen followed Tanya from the bed. Together, they stepped from the circle of protection and headed toward the bathroom. When they opened the door, they found the room full of steam, and written in the condensation on the mirror was the word *LEAVE*.

"I'm afraid to use the toilet," Tanya said as she did a little dance.

"It's morning now," Ellen said. "It doesn't have as much power in the daylight, remember?"

Tanya, unable to hold it a moment longer, scurried to the toilet. Ellen remained in the room with her but turned around, to give Tanya privacy.

"Do you think it's the same ghost that threatened you on our first night here?" Tanya asked from the commode.

"I have no idea."

Sue appeared at the door. "I always suspected the two of you might be having a lesbian fling."

When she saw the writing on the mirror, her mouth dropped open. "Did either of you do that? Are you trying to scare me? Because it's working."

"I wish it was a joke," Ellen said. "Tanya thinks it could be a message from the same ghost that bothered me on our first night."

"Or, it could be the doctor," Tanya said. "Maybe he followed us from the hospital grounds."

"I have an idea," Sue said. "But we'll have to wait for nightfall."

As they waited for their Big Dam Breakfast downstairs in the hotel restaurant, Ellen and her friends were glued to their phones. Ellen texted Chief Needham. Tanya researched Doctor Anthony Bridgewater. Sue researched more on Ferris Kahn.

"Chief Needham wants to know if we can come by the station sometime today," Ellen said.

Sue took a sip of her coffee. "Let's get it over with this morning, so we can return to our rooms for a nap. I didn't get a lick of sleep."

Ellen and Tanya giggled.

"What? I didn't."

"You could have fooled us," Ellen said.

"Oh, listen to this." Tanya stared at her phone. "'Six Companies managed to straddle the line between a private consortium of companies and a federal entity. As a private business, it profited immensely from its various enterprises surrounding the Hoover Dam—the commissary, the department store, the cafeteria, housing, transportation, and, most significantly, the hospital. As a federal contractor, Six Companies considered itself exempt from paying state taxes and undergoing state mining inspections. However, it also managed to escape federal restrictions.' Oh, here's the important part: 'A team of doctors employed by Six Companies and led by Dr. Anthony Bridgewater should have been, some would argue, on the federal payroll and susceptible to government policy, regulations, and inspections; however, the Bureau of Reclamation argued that since most of the residents in Boulder City were employees of Six Companies, it was the responsibility of Six Companies to build the hospital and employ its staff. This, some argue, created an overt conflict of interest that may have easily led down a path of corruption.'"

"May have," Ellen repeated. "It sounds as if the history books don't report corruption but only hint at it."

"I found something, too," Sue said before taking a sip of her coffee. "This is from a book by Michael Hilzik: 'MacDonald and Kahn were suspected of bribing a Los Angeles city official during a municipal construction dispute to obtain a settlement for a million dollars. Los Angeles investigators discovered that a large sum of money had been withdrawn from the bank account of MacDonald and Kahn on the same day that the city official, Sidney T. Graves, deposited an identical sum into his personal account. When the investigators sought access to MacDonald and Kahn's books, the books had mysteriously disappeared. At the time of this discovery, Alan MacDonald and Ferris Kahn had already moved across state lines to Nevada to begin construction on the Hoover Dam as part of Six Companies.'"

"So, Kahn may have been a criminal on the run before he ever arrived here," Ellen said.

"It's possible," Sue said. "But again, this book only hints at corruption. It doesn't prove it."

Just then, the waitress arrived with their order. Famished, Ellen took in the aroma and appearance of the fluffy pancakes, fried eggs, crispy bacon, and hashbrowns with pleasure. She and her friends said very little for the next several minutes.

But Ellen hadn't made that much progress with her breakfast when her phone dinged.

"It's Chief Needham," Ellen said. "He wants to know if we can be at the station in an hour."

"Works for me," Sue said.

"Sure," Tanya agreed.

When Ellen followed Tanya and Sue into the Boulder City Police Department, she felt a chill run down her back. She brushed off the uneasiness, chalking it up to exhaustion. She and her friends had been working almost nonstop and hadn't managed to get good rest in three days.

A police officer escorted Ellen and her friends down the hall to the conference room. Although Chief Needham wasn't there, the police officer assured them that he would arrive in a few minutes. Ellen and her friends were told to help themselves to coffee.

Even though she was full, Ellen poured herself a cup of coffee—all three of them did. Sue's idea of a nap before lunch was sounding better and better to Ellen.

They could hear the chief coming down the hall, due to his familiar cough.

"Good morning," Chief Needham said as he entered the room carrying a manila envelope. "How are you ladies this morning?"

"Tired," Tanya said.

"Believe me," the chief said before coughing into the crook of his arm. "I can relate."

As the chief took his seat at the head of the table, Sue relayed what had happened at the McGinty residence the previous night.

"And Erin felt better?" he asked with his brows lifted.

"Mary Jane later texted me that her sister-in-law and nephews were also cured of the Phantom Flu," Ellen added.

The chief leapt to his feet. "Wonderful news! Can you do the same for me?"

"We were thinking of doing a crossover ceremony at the cemetery," Tanya said. "So, we wouldn't have to do it forty-eight times."

"The Boulder City Municipal Cemetery?" the chief asked.

"Is that where the dam workers are buried?" Ellen asked.

"I don't think so," Chief Needham said before coughing into the crook of his arm. "I don't believe that cemetery had been established by then."

"Then where are the dam workers buried?" Sue asked.

"I believe St. Thomas, which was relocated to Overton in 1935, to avoid being flooded by Lake Mead."

"The bodies were exhumed and relocated?" Tanya said as she glanced from Sue to Ellen. "Oh, my God."

"No wonder James McGinty was lost," Ellen said. "He was unjustly diagnosed, his family deprived of workmen's comp, and then, a few years later, his place of rest was relocated."

"And then the hospital where he died was demolished," Sue added.

"Thank God he's at peace now," Tanya said. "But how will we help the others? I really can't see us going door to door."

"What if we bring all the victims of the Phantom Flu together in one place?" Ellen suggested. "If our theory is correct, and the flu is caused by spirit attachments, the afflicted will bring the spirits of their ancestors with them."

Sue turned to Chief Needham. "Does Boulder City have a convention center or a similar building large enough to accommodate 500 people?"

"We have a Civic Area," Needham said. "I can arrange to have everyone there as early as tomorrow evening. Would that work?"

"All we can do is try," Tanya said.

"Fantastic. And how long will it take for us to know if it worked?"

"Erin McGinty felt it immediately," Tanya said.

"So, if I'm still coughing my head off the next morning, we'll have our answer."

"Correct," Ellen said.

"Alrighty then," he said. "Fingers crossed."

"Fingers and toes," Sue said. "Just to be sure."

The chief laughed. "Fingers and toes."

He opened the manila folder and pulled out a photograph of a young man who appeared to be in his late twenties. The man had short red hair, brown eyes, and freckles on his cheeks.

"This is Martin McCready, the man whose body you discovered at the old hospital grounds."

"He looks much better in *that* picture than the one Ellen showed me," Sue said.

Ellen closed her eyes and shook her head.

"I'm sorry," Sue said. "I guess I'm a little nervous."

"I understand," the chief said. "But you have no reason to be nervous."

He took another photo from the envelope. "This is Hunter Merton, the man who dug up Martin McCready's body, dismembered it, and used a cat to leave his message."

The photo depicted another young man, probably in his mid to late thirties, with blond hair and blue eyes.

"Poor cat," Tanya murmured.

"According to Hunter, he found the cat dead on the side of the road."

"Did he say why he did it?" Sue asked.

"He says he doesn't know," the chief said. "I was hoping you ladies would talk to him."

Ellen's stomach did a flipflop. "Us? You want *us* to talk to him?"

"You don't have to, if you aren't comfortable."

"I'll do it," Sue said. She glanced at Ellen.

"I suppose we could talk to him," Ellen said.

Tanya clutched her *gris gris* bag. "Only if we place ourselves inside a circle of protection."

CHAPTER FOURTEEN

Hunter Merton

Before taking Ellen and her friends to the interrogation room to speak with Hunter Merton, Chief Needham lowered a projection screen in the conference room and showed a video of Merton's confession.

In the video, Merton held his head in his hands and wore a look of horror on his face. His blue eyes had dark circles beneath them. His blond hair looked oily, unwashed. His face was unshaven. And his lips trembled, like a junkie in need of a fix.

"Say it again," the chief, who sat across from Merton, said. "Say it for the camera."

"I did it," Merton said. "I cut up the body and carried it up the hill to 701 Park Place."

"When?"

"Last night."

"Why did you do it?"

"I don't know."

The chief paused, wearing a look of horror on his face that mirrored Merton's. "When did you get the idea to do this thing?"

"I don't know. It seems like a nightmare," Merton said. "Like I was sleepwalking the whole time."

"What time was it when you left your house?"

"I can barely remember leaving it."

"Do you remember taking the shovel from your garage?"

"Now that you mention it, I do."

"Do you remember driving to the cemetery?"

"Yes. Barely. It feels like a dream."

The chief asked, "How did you know where to find McCready's body?"

"It didn't matter whose body it was."

"Then why did you choose McCready?"

"I didn't choose him. I just went to the freshest grave—the one with the softest dirt."

"There are over three thousand graves in that cemetery. How did you know which one had the softest dirt?"

Merton shrugged. "I don't know. I just did."

"Then what happened."

"I dug up the casket and removed the body. It was heavier than I expected. I cut it into a few pieces, so it would be easier to haul into the back of my pickup."

The chief cringed. "And you felt nothing? No remorse for desecrating a man's body?"

"Like I said, I thought I was dreaming. I felt like I was outside of my body, watching—like someone else had taken over."

The chief stood up and paused the video in the conference room and said to Ellen and her friends, "That statement there. That's why I want you to talk to him. He said he felt like someone else had taken over. Do you ladies believe that's possible?"

"Oh, absolutely," Tanya said.

"Can this happen to anyone?" the chief asked. "Can it happen to me?"

Ellen sucked in her lips, searching for the right words. Sue and Tanya seemed to be doing the same.

"I guess your silence answers that question."

"Here's the thing, Chief," Ellen began. "You likely already have a spirit attached to you, right? Just like Erin did."

"My grandfather."

"Exactly," Sue said. "So, it's unlikely that this other, evil, spirit would possess someone who already has an attachment."

"And if your grandfather were to possess you," Tanya began, "it would make you sick, but it's unlikely that he would make you do evil things."

The chief seemed relieved. "The sooner you ladies can help the ghosts to crossover, the better. And this city will be indebted to you, I assure you."

"Well," Sue said, "let's not get ahead of ourselves."

The chief unpaused the video, in which he was asking Merton, "What did you do after you loaded the body into your truck?"

"I drove to 701 Park Place."

"Why did you choose that location?"

"I didn't. I just went there, without thinking about it. The address kept playing over and over in my mind, like a recording on a loop—701 Park Place, 701 Park Place."

"What did you do once you got there?" the chief asked.

"I carried the body parts, along with a dead cat I had found on the side of the road, up to the top of the hill. I laid the man's body where it seemed it was supposed to be."

"What do you mean by that statement—you laid the man's body where it seemed it was supposed to be?"

"I don't really know. It felt right. That's all I know."

"Then what did you do?"

"I ripped off the cat's head and spilled its blood on the cement slab beside the body. When the warm blood ran down my arm, it kind of woke me up. I saw what I had done, and I flung the cat from my hand in disgust and ran back to my truck. I hadn't driven very far when I pulled over and threw up on the side of the road. I went home and took a hot shower, put on fresh clothes, and went to sleep, exhausted and confused and not sure if what had happened was real. But when I heard about it on the news the next day, well, I was horrified. I knew I had to turn myself in."

Hunter Merton broke down into tears. "I don't know why I did it, but I did."

The chief stopped the video and said to Ellen and her friends, "Are you ready to talk to him?"

Ellen wondered how things had come to this—that she and her best friends would be asked by the chief of police to interrogate a man who'd mutilated a corpse.

"Can we have a minute to prepare ourselves?" Sue asked.

"Sure, you can." The chief stepped from the room, closing the door behind him.

"I don't think I can do this," Tanya admitted.

"None of us has to do anything we don't want to do," Ellen said.

"I want to talk to him," Sue said. "I think he was possessed, and I want to ask him if he sensed anyone. Maybe he'll give us a clue."

"I'll go with you," Ellen said. "We'll make a circle of protection."

"Now you're making me look bad," Tanya complained.

"You have to do what you feel comfortable doing," Ellen reassured her. "We haven't gone through a spirit attachment, so it's probably easier for us."

Tears flooded Tanya's eyes. "You sure you don't mind if I sit this one out? I'm not letting you down?"

Sue squeezed Tanya's hand. "You aren't letting us down."

Ellen hugged Tanya from behind. "Of course not."

Tanya sighed as a shudder shook her whole body. "Thanks, guys."

Ellen opened the door of the conference room and found the chief waiting in the hall.

"Sue and I are ready. Tanya's going to sit this one out."

"I understand," Chief Needham said. "Please, follow me. Tanya? You can sit with me and watch, if you'd like."

A few minutes later, Ellen and Sue entered the interrogation room, where Hunter Merton was already seated, handcuffed, in a metal folding chair in front of a metal table, that was bolted to the floor. She and Sue each took a shaker of salt and made a ring of protection around the table before they returned the shakers to their purses and sat in the chairs across the table from Hunter. To their right was a one-way mirror, behind which Needham and Tanya were watching.

"What are you doing?" Hunter asked.

Hunter's eyes were red, and his face was twisted with despair. Ellen was no longer afraid of him. She felt sorry for him. She could feel his confusion, despair, and sorrow.

"Hello, Hunter. I'm Sue, and this is my friend, Ellen."

"Hi," Ellen said.

"What's the deal with the salt?" he asked.

"We'll explain later," Ellen said. "For now, we just want to talk."

"Are you my lawyers?"

"No. We aren't your lawyers," Sue said. "Although I always did think I'd make a good lawyer. My mom used to say I could talk anyone into doing just about anything."

"That's true," Ellen said with a laugh. "Sue can be pretty persuasive."

"I've already confessed," Hunter said. "There's no need to play good cop and…good cop, or whatever this is."

Ellen fell into a fit of giggles. He actually thought they were cops?

Sue was soon giggling, too.

"I'm sorry," Sue said. "We're a little nervous." She glanced at the one-way mirror. "I wonder if we can get any snacks."

"Sue, we just had breakfast."

"But I'm a nervous eater."

"We said we were going to count calories."

"No one, not even God, would expect me to do that under these circumstances," Sue chastised.

"Who are you ladies?" Hunter asked. "Why are you here?"

Ellen realized in that moment that interrogation was not her or Sue's strong point.

"We're paranormal investigators," Sue said. "And we want to ask you a few questions about some of the strange feelings you had while you were committing the crimes you confessed to."

"*Paranormal* investigators? Like ghost hunters?"

"Something like that," Ellen said.

Sue cleared her throat. "Now then, you said you felt as if you were sleepwalking, or outside of your body, watching, as if someone else had taken over, right?"

"Right."

"Can you recall anything else about how you felt?" Sue asked.

"For example," Ellen began, "did you notice any smells? Or did you feel sick to your stomach or have a headache?"

"I had a bad headache," Hunter said. "And, now that you mention it, I remember smelling sulfur."

Sue and Ellen glanced at one another.

"That's interesting," Ellen said.

"Why?" Hunter asked.

"When you snapped out of it and realized what was happening," Sue said, "did you feel differently?"

"I don't know. I think I was too freaked out to feel anything."

"Does your head still ache?" Ellen asked.

"No. I guess not."

"Can you remember when the headache went away?" Sue asked.

"No. I don't know. Maybe as I was driving home. I'm not sure."

"Did you smell sulfur as you were driving away?" Ellen asked.

"I can't remember. I don't think so."

"Can you smell it now?" Ellen asked.

"No."

"Did you hear any voices, other than your own, inside you head?" Sue asked.

"I'm not crazy."

"I'm not saying you are," Sue said. "Not everyone who hears voices is mentally ill."

"Well, now that you mention it, the address that was playing inside my head—701 Park Place—didn't sound like my voice or my thought."

"What did it sound like?" Sue asked just as Ellen was about to.

"It was a man's voice. He had a little bit of an accent."

Ellen lifted her brows in surprise. "Can you describe it or imitate it?"

"It reminded me of a documentary I watched a long time ago about FDR. It sounded like Franklin Roosevelt's voice."

Sue and Ellen frowned. Ellen doubted the ghost of FDR had possessed Hunter Merton, but maybe it was a spirit from the same time period.

Ellen bit her lip. "Hunter, were you born in Boulder City?"

"Yes."

"Did your ancestors reside here during the construction of the Hoover Dam?" Ellen asked.

"Yes."

"What were those ancestors' names?" Sue asked.

"Anthony and Clara Bridgewater, and their children, Thomas and John Bridgewater."

Ellen's mouth fell open. Sue's eyes looked like they might pop right out of their sockets.

"Why?" Hunter asked. "Why is that important?"

"We aren't sure yet," Sue explained.

Ellen reached out and touched Hunter's hands, which rested in cuffs on the table. "Just know that we believe you and will do all that we can to help you."

Tears streamed from Hunter's tired, swollen eyes. "Thank you."

The door to the interrogation room opened, and Chief Needham motioned for Sue and Ellen to join him in the hall. He glanced at Merton before closing the door and turning to Ellen.

"Never touch a suspect," the chief said.

The blood rushed to Ellen's cheeks. "I'm sorry."

Sue put her hands on her hips, warrior ready. "How was she supposed to know that? You didn't give us any instructions before sending us in there as a *favor* to you."

"You're right." The chief sighed. "Please accept my apologies, Ellen, Sue. I'm grateful. You're right. It's my fault for not telling you." The chief coughed into the crook of his arm.

"No worries," Ellen said.

"Thank you. I have just one more question: Why are Merton's ancestors relevant to this investigation? Do you think they're haunting him? Possessing him?"

Sue dropped her arms to her side. "It's possible that Dr. Bridgewater's ghost used his descendant to communicate a message to us."

"Hunter claims to have no memory of writing the message in the blood," the chief said.

"Maybe Brian did see a shadow man," Ellen said. "Maybe it was Bridgewater."

"Do you think the doctor is seeking redemption?" Tanya, who had joined them in the hallway, asked.

"*I did as I was told,*" Ellen repeated. "His message sounds defensive, not remorseful."

"When you do that ceremony, that…what's it called again?" the chief asked.

"Crossover ceremony," Sue said.

"Yes. That. When you do that crossover ceremony tomorrow night in the Civic Area, will that help Bridgewater's ghost to move on, too?"

Ellen frowned as she glanced at her friends. "Only if he's ready."

CHAPTER FIFTEEN

Hotel Ghosts

In the dead of night, when the rest of the Boulder Dam Hotel was dark and quiet, Ellen, Sue, and Tanya, crept through the hall from Sue's room with arms full of equipment and rode the elevator down to the still lobby.

Among the sleeping furniture before the empty fireplace, Tanya set up a full-spectrum camera on its tripod, while Ellen situated the electromagnetic pump nearby and turned it on. Sue noted the temperature and EMF readings—the former being exceptionally low for the middle of the summer at 60 degrees and the latter being exceptionally high at 2 milliGauss. These readings made Ellen and her friends suspect that the lobby ghost was already there, without needing to be summoned.

While Sue recorded their baseline readings, Ellen poured a thin line of salt around the furniture grouping. Then they made themselves comfortable on the couches.

Ellen had been about to address the spirit realm when the familiar voice of a young woman startled her.

"Hello, dears."

As usual, it was a disembodied voice of a young woman that came from the darkness of the lobby.

"Hello," Ellen said, still wondering if it might be possible that other paranormal investigators were playing tricks on Ellen and her friends. "Thank you for joining us."

"It's you who have joined me, is it not?"

"Yes. You're right," Sue said. "You'll have to excuse us. We're not very bright."

"On the contrary," the disembodied voice continued. "Compared to me, you're a picture of perfect luminosity."

"You're a witty one, aren't you?" Tanya said.

"I see you've joined the ranks of the night people."

Tanya glanced at Ellen and Sue. "I suppose I have."

"Good for you. Now, let's make this quick. I can't stay for long."

Before Ellen could ask the ghost to explain, Sue said, "Would you mind telling us your name?"

"I don't mind at all. It's Edna Jackson."

"That's a lovely name," Ellen said.

"There's no need to suck up, dear."

Ellen chuckled. "What should we call you? Miss Jackson?"

"Edna, please."

"Edna," Sue began. "When were you born?"

"In 1899."

"What brought you here, to Boulder City?" Tanya asked.

"I came from Idaho, where I was a schoolteacher, to marry my love, who worked as a surveyor for the Bureau of Reclamation. I left the snow patches in Idaho for the 104-degree heat and the love of my life. I was only twenty years old."

"Was it worth it?" Sue asked.

The disembodied voice of Edna Jackson laughed. "Despite the centipedes, the scorpions, the tarantulas, and the snakes, which were my constant companions, and the torrid heat that radiated off the canyon walls and squeezed every bit of fluid from my body, I was enthralled by the herds of bighorn sheep and by the willows that danced over the riverbeds and by the magnificence of the narrow gorge, with its castle-like walls of rock. I could gaze out at the canyon for hours, finding new shapes in the rock formations, like I used to do with the clouds in Idaho."

"Sounds like you were in your element," Ellen said.

"I wish that were true," Edna said. "Unfortunately, the desert is no one's element. Soon after I arrived and married my beau, we were stranded here, near the canyon, and our food and supplies quickly dwindled. My husband set off for the borax factory on foot, leaving me with a partially filled canteen of water, a can of peaches, and two lemons, and I never saw him again."

"How awful," Tanya said. "Why didn't you go with him?"

"Jack was afraid for me to make the journey in my condition. You see, I'm expecting our child."

"Why haven't you moved on?" Sue asked. "Why do you remain at this hotel?"

"My dear Jack told me to wait for him," she said. "I'm afraid that, if I go, I won't see him again."

Ellen was about to tell the ghost of Edna Jackson that her husband had likely moved on, and that she would find him on the other side, but before she could say that, Edna said, "And now that you've heard my story, shall we get to the real reason why you're here?"

"The real reason?" Tanya repeated.

"You want to know about the soul that followed you here."

"Yes," Sue said. "Did he come from the old Boulder City Hospital grounds?"

"I believe he followed you from Hoover Dam, but that's only a guess, because of the way he smells."

"Is he good or evil?" Tanya asked.

"He's angry and doesn't want you here."

Ellen wondered if Edna was talking about Dr. Bridgewater or Ferris Kahn.

"Is he still here, at this hotel?" Sue asked.

"Oh, yes. I'm looking at him now. I'm not sure if he can hear me, but he seems to be able to hear you."

Ellen sat up and sucked in air. "He's here *now*? In *this room*?"

"Try not to make me repeat myself, dear. I need to get back soon."

"To where?" Ellen asked.

"To my meeting place with Jack. He could be coming along at any moment."

"This other ghost that is here with us," Sue said. "Can you tell us his name or what he looks like?"

"There are many souls in the room with us," she said, "but none so focused on you as he. I don't know his name. He won't speak with me. He doesn't speak with any of us. His soul has become unrecognizable, as if it's been twisted by guilt and shame and pride. He looks like a demon but acts like a gentleman—one above me and the rest of us in station."

"How many souls are with you, Edna?" Sue asked.

"Currently, I count six. The others have been here for a long, long time, but this one just arrived. He followed you here."

"Do you know what he wants?" Tanya asked.

"He wants you to leave, to stop meddling, to go home."

"Do you know if he was responsible for what Hunter Merton did to the body of Martin McCready?"

"No. And now I must go, dears. Perhaps I'll see you again tomorrow night."

"Wait! Please!" Sue cried.

"Edna? Are you there?" Ellen asked.

"Edna?" Tanya said. "If you're still here, can you give us a sign?"

In a lower voice, Ellen asked Sue and Tanya, "Should we try to engage with the other ghost. The one Edna said is focused on us?"

"I don't know," Tanya said. "He sounds pretty scary."

"It may be the only way to get to the bottom of this case," Sue said. "I think we should try. I have more holy water in my purse, if things get out of hand."

"What's the temperature now?" Ellen asked Sue.

"Sixty-two degrees. And the EMF readings are still high."

"Do you think this ghost could be Ferris Kahn?" Tanya asked.

At that moment, the sconce over the stairs flickered.

Ellen sucked in her lips. "I think it's possible. If he followed us here from Hoover Dam, he could have followed us to the McGinty residence."

"And then, when I banished him from there, he could have returned here, to the last place he'd been."

Tanya pulled out her phone. "Thank goodness there's still a charge. Why don't we see what more we can learn about him before we try to interact with him?"

Ellen sighed. "We don't even know if that's who's with us."

"We could ask him," Tanya said.

"And he could lie," Sue pointed out.

"I just found his obituary," Tanya said. "He doesn't sound like he was a bad man. He had a wife and two daughters."

The light above the stairwell flickered again.

"Having a family doesn't make you a good person," Ellen said.

"True," Sue said. "Tanya has a family, and she can be downright mean."

"Sue," Ellen scolded.

"I'm just trying to lighten the mood."

"We may as well try to reach out to him," Tanya said. "If we don't confront this ghost now, he may keep following us wherever we go, and the last thing I want is to take him home with me."

"Good point," Ellen said. She turned to Sue. "Ready?"

Sue took a deep breath and exhaled. Then she nodded and said, "Spirits of the other realm, we mean you no harm. We come in peace. Is anyone here with us? If so, please give us a sign."

The sconce over the stairs flickered again.

"Do you think that was a sign?" Tanya whispered.

"Possibly," Sue murmured. Then in a louder voice, she said, "Was that you, spirit? If you made the light flicker, please do it again."

The light flickered and went out. Only a dim lamp on the front desk on the other side of the lobby and the soft rays of moonlight through the front windows provided any light in the room.

"It could have been a bad bulb," Ellen pointed out.

"Spirit?" Sue continued. "If you caused that light to go out, can you give us another sign?"

They heard a knock from somewhere above them. Although it could be explained by another hotel guest moving around, Sue asked, "Was that you, spirit? Is so, please knock once for yes or twice for no."

A single knock.

"Yes," Tanya whispered.

"Spirit?" Sue continued. "Is your name Ferris Kahn? Please knock once for yes or twice for no."

A single knock.

"Yes," Tanya whispered.

"Mr. Kahn?" Sue asked. "We mean you no harm. We want to help you find peace. Will you let us help you? Please knock once for yes or twice for no."

Two knocks.

"No," Tanya whispered.

"Now what?" Ellen wondered.

"I don't know," Sue said. "Any ideas, Tanya?"

"Not really. Maybe we can't resolve this. Maybe we should try to banish him, and hope he flies back to Hoover Dam."

Knocks hammered the walls and ceilings as it had the previous night at the McGinty residence, sounding like hail. Sue grabbed the holy water from her purse and flung water outside of their circle of protection.

"Ghost of Ferris Kahn! I rebuke you from this hotel in the name of Abraham! In the name of Moses! I rebuke you in the name of Elijah! In the name of Jesus! I rebuke you, Ferris Kahn, in the name of Mohammed! I rebuke you in the name of God, our Father, almighty, who created Heaven and Earth! Fly away, evil spirit! Fly away, never to return!"

The knocking ceased. Ellen looked up to find an audience had assembled at the top of the stairs. Several onlookers were using their phones to video-record and take photos. After the hush of silence following Sue's incantation, the onlookers clapped their hands and cheered Ellen and her friends. Someone even whistled while another shouted, "Way to go, Ghost Healers!"

Ellen and her friends smiled. Then they busted out laughing. Even though it was a small victory, it felt good to be recognized for it. As they packed up their equipment, a few of the hotel guests came downstairs to ask questions. Sue said that while they were too tired to discuss anything with them tonight, they should watch the news and social media outlets for an announcement from Chief Needham.

"Are you referring to the gathering at the Civic Area tomorrow night?" one young man with a face full of freckles asked them.

"Yes," Ellen said. "Plan to attend. All will be explained then."

The young people offered to help Ellen, Sue, and Tanya to carry their equipment, but worried there might be a catch, the three friends declined the offers.

Once they were upstairs and finally free of their audience, the three friends decided to take their chances by sleeping in their own beds. Hopefully, Sue's incantation had driven anything evil from the hotel—at least for the night.

Ellen changed into her pajamas and collapsed into bed. Just as she was about to fall asleep, she thought she heard someone whisper, "Coward."

CHAPTER SIXTEEN

The Afflicted

Ellen spent most of Thursday in her hotel room sleeping and re-laxing. She watched *Mama Mia! Here We Go Again*, which made her laugh out loud but left her in tears. She'd forgotten about the sad moment in the church with Meryl Streep playing a ghost. It had reminded Ellen of Paul.

She knew her husband had passed on and was in a better place. She would have sensed his presence otherwise; however, she also wondered if he was looking down on her and was aware of what she was doing with her life.

More importantly, she wondered if he was aware of her relationship with Brian, and, if so, how it made Paul feel. She had once called their marriage of thirty plus years a sham, but it had been a far cry from that. They hadn't been a perfect couple—if such a thing existed. Maybe she would have been happier if she had left him, or maybe she would have been miserable without him. She'd never know. But she did know that she loved him, had built a family with him, and had lived a life with him, and she always, no matter how many years she outlived him, would feel connected to him.

Tears flooded her eyes.

"Oh, Paul," she whispered. "I miss you."

She buried her face in her hands and allowed herself a good cry. She didn't cry over Paul's death often, and, when she did, it came hard, like a tidal wave washing over an entire village. Her body shuddered until she was gasping for air—hyperventilating, she soon realized.

Lifting her arms over her head, she took in a deep, slow, breath, trying to calm herself down. Then she slowly exhaled, being sure to press the air completely out of her lungs, as her therapist had taught her. Once her breathing was back to normal, she got up, walked around the room, and picked up the tray of empty lunch plates from earlier and laid it in the hall outside her door. Then she collapsed on the sofa with the television remote and looked for another uplifting movie or show to watch, to pass the time until dinner.

Just before dusk, Ellen, Sue, and Tanya stood beside Chief Needham and Mayor McManius and a chaplain by the name of Carl Swenson, who served at a local church. The six of them congregated behind a portable stage that had been set up with sound equipment, spotlights, and colorful pennant banners. On the opposite side of the stage, a crowd of well over a thousand people had gathered, at the Civic Area in Boulder City known as Frank T. Crowe Memorial Park. The park was too small for the number in attendance, but the people in the crowd didn't seem to care. They had squeezed together like packaged hotdogs, waiting to hear the mayor's announcement about the Phantom Flu.

Many of the people were coughing, but Ellen could tell by the hopeful looks on their faces that word had spread about the possibility of a cure.

At seven thirty, the lights on the stage came on, and the people in the crowd silenced themselves as Mayor McManius took the stage. He stood before a microphone and cleared his throat.

"City officials, citizens, and guests of Boulder City, thank you for joining me tonight for this important, unprecedented occasion. I think I'm safe in calling it that, for nothing like this has ever happened in the history of our city."

Many people in the crowd nodded. Someone shouted, "Amen!"

The mayor chuckled and said, "Speaking of Amens, please help me welcome Chaplain Carl Swenson to the stage, where he will lead us in a moment of prayer."

As applause rang out over the darkening park, the chaplain joined the mayor on the stage.

"Thank you, Mayor McManius. Thank you, citizens and guests of this city, for that warm welcome. Please, bow your heads."

The chaplain waited while men removed their hats and caps, and everyone bowed their heads in silence.

"Dear God, our Heavenly guide, please be with us tonight as we attempt to bring you glory and your children peace through this crossover celebration. We ask that you protect us from evil and shower us with your love and mercy. We pray to you in faith, dear God. Amen."

Many in the audience replied, "Amen."

"Thank you, Chaplain," the mayor said before Carl Swenson exited the stage.

"At this time," Kiernan said, addressing the crowd, "I'd like to invite our Chief of Police, Brent Needham, to the stage to explain to you what will happen tonight. Please welcome Chief Needham."

The chief winked at Ellen and her friends before he left them behind the stage to join the mayor.

"Thank you, Mayor, and all of you here tonight at Frank T. Crowe Memorial Park for this important historic moment," Chief Needham said before he coughed into the crook of his arm. "As some of you may have heard, a well-known team of paranormal investigators has come to our great city to help us in our time of need. They have already proven their mettle by uncovering significant discrepancies in records dating back to the time of the construction of Hoover Dam, bringing to our attention that at least forty-eight dam builders were issued fraudulent death certificates citing pneumonia as the cause of death when they were likely killed by carbon monoxide poisoning."

Gasps filled the air, and people in the crowd began to converse with one another as they processed this new information.

"If I can have your attention once again, good citizens of Boulder City," the chief said, "I have more to say."

He waited for the crowd to quiet down. He coughed and cleared his throat. Then he motioned to four people standing near the front of the audience to join him on stage. Ellen recognized Erin McGinty and supposed the other three were her aunt and cousins.

The chief confirmed her suspicions when he said, "Those of you who know Erin McGinty and her aunt Paula Meyer and cousins Tina and Jennifer Meyer also know that, like many of us, they suffered from the Phantom Flu for months."

People in the crowd nodded.

"How do you ladies feel now?" Chief Needham asked them.

Paula Meyer stepped in front of the mic, and, with tears in her eyes, shouted, "We feel great!"

The audience exploded with applause.

As Erin and her relatives stepped down from the stage, Chief Needham said, "The people responsible for their recovery are here with us this evening. Please welcome Sue Graham, Ellen Mohr, and Tanya Sanchez of Ghost Healers, Inc."

Ellen followed Tanya and Sue onto the stage. She felt nervous for so many reasons. First, she had never spoken to such a large group of people before. Second, the crossover ceremony might not work as it had at the McGinty residence. And finally, she had a bad feeling that something evil might try to sabotage their efforts to help the ghosts of the Hoover Dam victims move on.

Beyond those three main concerns was the fact that a crowd this large could not be protected by a ring of salt or the smoke of a sage smudge stick. It was highly possible that, in their efforts to help those afflicted by the Phantom Flu, Ellen and her friends would make everyone present vulnerable to spirit possessions.

Sue, the bravest of the three, stepped up to the microphone. "Thank you, Boulder City, for entrusting us with this ceremony. We want you to know that we come with good hearts and the best of intentions, but we cannot guarantee that we will be successful. However, the likelihood of our success can be exponentially increased by your participation. If you could please take the hand of the person on either side of you, to symbolize our unity, this will give us strength against anything malicious attempting to undermine our efforts."

Sue reached out and joined hands with Ellen and Tanya. Ellen, in turn, took the chief's hand, and Tanya took Kiernan's. The chaplain returned to the stage to join hands with the chief.

Sue let go of Ellen's hand to put on her readers before taking the list of the forty-eight dam workers who'd been wrongly recorded as having died of pneumonia in the early 1930s. As Sue held the paper in front of her, Ellen held Sue's wrist to keep the symbolism of unity unbroken.

"Spirits of the other realm," Sue began. "We are here in peace to help you to find your way to the other side. We ask you to release your loved one, so their health may be restored, and to pass to the other side, knowing that the wrong against you has been acknowledged and recorded in human history. Never again will the people who flock to see the beauty of the Hoover Dam neglect to count you among the number of workers who sacrificed themselves so that the desert might bloom."

Sue seemed to be struggling to clear her throat.

"Are you okay?" Ellen whispered.

"My throat is raw," she whispered back. "Can you continue in my place?"

Ellen took Sue's readers and the list of the forty-eight men. Sue grabbed ahold of Ellen's wrist. Then Ellen spoke into the mic:

"Oh, spirits, I call you by name and invite you to release your loved ones and pass to the other side, where other loved ones await you. I call on F.H. Wolff, H. Needham, William. H. Minton, Charles C. Cliff, William Dorr, and E.F. McCarthy to pass into the light. I call on C.L. Allen,

Phillip A. Lowe, E.C. Rowe, Harold Rex, Martin Ostrom, John McMaster, R. D. Creighton, M.C. Van Rader, Walter Long, Norman Baker, Frank Holtry, Bert Sanford, A.W. McCready, and George Overgard to cross over to the light. I call on Jack Stacey, Jacob Ruterman, G.C. Baker, L.A. Katch, G.D. Farnsworth, A.J. Winkler, Paul C. Sharitz, and William Garl to pass over to the other side. I call on Harry Gilbert, Fred J. Scott, Charles King, Sam Rather, J.W. Pinckard, Raymond Allen, Henry Fisher, William Sutton, J.N. Slick, Alton M. King, Roy Drake, Frank Vales, and N.C. Christopher to cross over to the light. I call on Frank Staehle, Harvey E. Bolich, William Stevens, Thomas Wood, Tom N. Hulsey, and Martin Kelly to find your way to the light."

That concluded the list of names, so Ellen added, "Those of you who have been afflicted with the Phantom Flu, I beseech you to personally ask your ancestor by name to leave you and to find peace on the other side."

Beside her, Chief Needham said, "Harold Needham, I beg you to leave me and to cross over into the light."

The chief flinched and released Ellen's hand.

"Are you okay?" she asked him.

At first a murmur and then a roar erupted in the crowd. Ellen and her friends watched anxiously as people prayed, sobbed, and shouted into the dark night for the spirits around them to find peace. Ellen felt a mixture of hope, love, and fear in the air. She prayed that no malicious spirit would interfere.

She turned back to the chief, who seemed to be in shock. The chaplain had taken hold of the chief's hand again.

"Brent?" he asked. "How do you feel?"

"Tired as hell. Sleepy. But…." He took in a deep breath. "I can breathe. I can breathe without coughing!"

Others in the crowd were wearing expressions of disbelief and gratitude. Numbers began to rush the stage as people shouted, "Thank you!", "We're healed!" and "It's a miracle!"

The chief, the mayor, and the chaplain helped Ellen and her friends from the stage and escorted them to the limo, where Kirk was waiting for them.

Ellen followed Sue and Tanya into the back of the vehicle to find a surprise waiting for her. Brian was waiting with a tray of margaritas.

"Sounds like it's time to celebrate," he said with a grin.

CHAPTER SEVENTEEN

Vegas, Baby

A trip to Vegas couldn't have come at a better time for the emotionally drained members of Ghost Healers, Inc. They spent three days attending shows, playing the slots, trying their hand at blackjack, drinking margaritas, and eating all kinds of rich and decadent foods.

As Sue reminded them more than once, even God wouldn't expect them to count calories after all that they'd been through.

On Sunday night, their last night there, after a hilarious comedy show that had left her in a joyful mood, Ellen joined Brian at the hot tub on the rooftop of their penthouse suite at ten o'clock, as had been their custom all weekend.

Beneath sexy, dark brows, his gray eyes sparkled in the moonlight. Rivulets glistened on his broad chest. He ran his fingers through his silver hair and gazed at her mouth. She leaned in and met his lips with hers.

He took her breath away, sending chills of pleasure all over her skin. Was it wrong for her to feel this way? It had been two years since Paul's passing. That seemed like such a long time on the one hand and like no time at all on the other.

She shook her head, trying to shake away the guilt that had been ruining moments like this one lately.

If Brian noticed her hesitation, he chose to ignore it when he smiled at her and said, "I have a surprise for you."

She smiled gleefully. "What is it?"

"You want me to blurt it out? You don't want to ask for hints and try to guess?"

"Is it bigger than a breadbox?"

"Much bigger."

"Please don't tell me you bought me my own private jet."

He threw his head back and laughed.

"Oh, no. Is that my surprise? You bought me a jet?"

He shook his head, still laughing. "I'll be sure to take that one off my list of possible Christmas gifts for you."

She laughed, too. "Okay, it's bigger than a breadbox. Is it bigger than a jet?"

"Considerably."

"What? Oh, my gosh, Brian! What is it?" Her stomach clenched a little. She hoped he hadn't bought a house for the two of them to live in together. She'd told him from the beginning that, as much as she loved him and enjoyed his company, she preferred to live alone.

"Look at your face!" he said with a grin. "You're terrified."

She rolled her eyes, shedding a few of her nerves. "You enjoy tormenting me, don't you!"

"I just love to watch the—what's the word—*range* of facial expressions that cross that beautiful face of yours."

"Well, I'm done guessing, because I don't believe you anymore," she teased.

"All right, all right. I'll come clean. After you told me your plan in Boulder City to get the whole community together for a crossover ceremony, it occurred to me that, if it worked—and I was pretty sure it would, knowing you—the community would be healed and the price of the old Boulder City Hospital estate would drive back up."

Ellen bent her brows, worried about where he was headed.

"Uh, oh," he said, picking up on her change in mood. "You don't look pleased."

"Did you buy the Boulder City Hospital property from underneath me?"

"What? No! I bought it *for* you."

She crossed her arms over her chest. "I can't believe you didn't talk to me about this first."

"I wanted to surprise you. Talking to you about it first would have ruined the element of surprise."

"I used to think I liked surprises, but the older I get, the more I realize I don't particularly enjoy them."

"You don't have to accept the gift," he said stiffly. "I can keep the property for myself."

"It doesn't matter, either way," she said.

"What do you mean by that?"

"You say it's a surprise for me, but we both know you bought it for yourself. This is something Paul never would have done. He always consulted with me on every major purchase, even if I didn't always reciprocate." Tears flooded her eyes.

"Need I say the obvious?"

She met his cold gaze. "The obvious?"

"My name is *Brian*, not Paul."

Brian flew out of Las Vegas to Portland early Monday morning, leaving Ellen feeling blue. Although she'd apologized for bringing up Paul, and Brian had said not to worry about it, the tension between them remained unresolved.

To make matters worse, he'd insisted on leaving Kirk behind to drive her and her friends around until their work was done in Boulder City.

The guilt on Ellen's heart felt like a vice.

She tried to hide her mood from her friends as they spent their final day taking in a show, eating extravagant food, and rolling the dice. But more than once, they asked her what was wrong.

"I'm just tired," she'd said.

But they'd had to pry her away from the slot machines. It must have been obvious to Sue and Tanya that something wasn't adding up. If Ellen was tired, why couldn't they get her to leave Vegas?

She supposed she wasn't the best actress in the world.

It was nearly one in the morning when Ellen finally agreed to follow them to the limo, where Kirk was waiting with their overnight bags already packed in the trunk.

They weren't on the road to Boulder City for long when Sue said to Ellen, "You've been moping around all day. You haven't been tired. You've been sad. What happened?"

"Brian bought me the old Boulder City Hospital estate."

Sue and Tanya's chins nearly hit the floorboards.

Sue leaned forward. "And that makes you sad because…"

"Because I don't like people making decisions for me. Because I think he just wanted the property for himself, so he could turn it into something like the Kennedy School. And because…" Tears filled her eyes. "Because if I were going to buy the hospital, I'd want it to be something we—the three of us—did together."

Tanya shook her head. "You know I love you, Ellen, but I think you're making a problem out of nothing. I'm not sure I would have agreed to buy it, anyway. I'm still freaked out over what we saw."

Ellen sucked in her lips and said nothing, though she disagreed with Tanya's claim that Ellen was making a problem out of nothing. Ellen felt like she was entering the final chapter of her life, and she wanted more control than she'd had in previous ones. She wanted clear boundaries between her and Brian. They were friends and lovers, but they weren't a *married couple*—not like she'd been with Paul. There would never be another man that would be to her what Paul had been. He was irreplaceable.

She struggled to keep her tears from tumbling down her cheeks.

"So, what are you going to do?" Sue asked her.

"I don't know."

"What's that?" Tanya pointed through the car window at a figure stumbling in the middle of the road about five minutes outside of Boulder City.

The figure appeared to be a young man, perhaps in his late twenties. He was dragging his feet, like he was either drunk or exhausted.

"Do you think that's the phantom the Blakes saw on the way back from Vegas a few weeks ago?" Sue asked with astonishment.

"I believe it is." Ellen lowered the window between the back and front of the limo. "Kirk, would you mind pulling over?"

"I guess our crossover ceremony didn't help *him*," Sue said.

Kirk stopped the car on the side of the road. They could still see the man stumbling in the headlights of the limo.

"We can't go after him," Tanya said. "If we want to help him to escape this constant loop he must be in, we can't go after him. It just makes him run away."

"Excuse me, ladies," Kirk said to them over his shoulder. "Am I to understand that the man in the road is a *ghost?*"

"We think so," Sue said.

"But might it be an actual person in need of our assistance?" Kirk asked.

Sue shrugged. "Only one way to find out."

"We need a circle of protection," Tanya said.

"How will we manage that in the limo?" Ellen asked.

"Easy," Sue said. "We'll sprinkle it around the outside."

Ellen cocked her head to the side. "We're going to reach out to him from inside of the limo?"

Sue lifted her palms. "Why not?"

Ellen sighed. "I don't have any better ideas. Let's give yours a whirl."

"We need to hurry," Sue said. "Another car could come by at any moment and frighten the spirit away."

Ellen, Sue, and Tanya quickly but quietly crept into the hot night, crouching close to the vehicle as they made a line of salt along its perimeter. Then they climbed back inside, carefully closed the doors, and rolled the windows down.

The hot air invaded the car. Ellen was surprised that the apparition continued to drag his feet in the road.

"Spirit of the other realm," Sue shouted through the window. "We mean you no harm. We want you to cross over into the light, so you can move on and find peace."

The apparition disappeared.

"Holy shit!" Kirk blurted out. He rubbed his eyes. "Holy shit!"

Ellen gaped. "I guess we were right."

Kirk made no reply as he stared at the beam of his headlights, where the apparition had once stood.

"Do you think he crossed over already?" Tanya asked. "That seemed too easy."

Sue pushed her bangs from her eyes. "I doubt it."

"Darn," Tanya said. "I was hoping we could help him."

"Just because we can't see him doesn't mean he isn't there," Ellen said. "Let's keep trying."

"Spirit of the other realm, we mean you no harm," Sue said again. "If you can hear us, please give us a sign."

The headlights of the limo flickered.

Kirk stiffened in his seat. "I'm not sure I want to be a part of this, Mrs. Mohr."

Ellen felt bad for not asking the driver's permission before beginning the séance. She shouldn't have assumed that he'd be okay with this. "My apologies, Kirk."

As she was about to tell him to continue to Boulder City, she was startled by the appearance of a face in her window.

Ellen, Sue, and Tanya screamed, which caused Kirk to jump in his seat.

"Holy shit," Kirk said again.

"Stay in the car," Tanya warned. "We're safe as long as we don't break the circle of protection."

The face vanished.

"Spirit!" Sue cried in a quivering voice. "We mean you no harm. What holds you here? Why can't you move on?"

The face appeared in the front windshield, scaring Kirk so badly that he almost jumped through the roof of the car. He slammed on the gas and the horn, skidded out onto the street, and zigzagged dangerously between the lanes.

"Kirk, calm down!" Ellen cried. "Easy! Easy!"

Kirk steadied the limo with trembling hands on the wheel.

"Are you okay, Kirk?" Sue asked. "Are you sure you shouldn't pull over?"

"I'm okay," he said, panting and clutching his chest. "I'm okay."

A few minutes later, they pulled in front of the Boulder Dam Hotel. Kirk, who had regained his composure, helped Ellen and her friends out of the vehicle and handed them their luggage from the trunk.

"Thank you," they said to Kirk.

"I'm sorry about tonight," Ellen added. "I shouldn't have gotten you involved."

"All in a good day's work," he said with a hint of sarcasm.

"Thanks again," she said.

As she followed Sue and Tanya toward the entrance of the hotel, Ellen glanced once more at Kirk as he was driving away.

The apparition of the stumbling young man appeared in the headlights. The phantom had followed them.

Kirk slammed on the breaks just as the ghost disappeared. Then Kirk sped away faster than he should have.

Not sure whether she should run toward or away from the spot where the specter had been, Ellen stood paralyzed near the curb.

In spite of the heat, she felt a chill crawl down her spine.

"Spirit of the other realm," she muttered, still unsure if reaching out to it was the right move. "I come in peace."

Sue and Tanya called out to her from the threshold of the hotel. "Ellen? Aren't you coming?"

"He followed us," she said. "I saw him. He's out here somewhere."

"Why don't we call it a night?" Tanya said. "We can always drive back to the place on the road where we first found him and try again."

"But I think he's here," Ellen said. "I think I can sense him. What if he doesn't go back to where he was? What if we made things worse?"

"I doubt things can get worse for a spirit who can't move on," Sue said.

"I'm going to bed," Tanya said.

"Come on, Ellen," Sue said. "It's late."

Reluctantly, Ellen turned away and followed her friends through the hotel entrance and into the quiet lobby.

The sconce over the stairs hadn't been fixed, so, except for the dim lamp at the front desk and the moonlight shining in through the windows, the lobby was dark. As on previous nights, there was no one manning the front desk, but as Ellen and her friends walked past it, they heard the young lobby ghost.

"Hello, dears," she said from the darkness. "Welcome back."

"Thank you, Edna," they said, pausing before the desk to speak with their favorite ghost.

"It's nice to be in the company of pleasant, courteous night people."

"Likewise," Sue replied.

"Who did you bring with you tonight?" Edna asked.

"Is someone with us?" Tanya asked. "Is it a young man dragging his feet?"

"Indeed," she said. "A handsome young man. He reminds me of....oh!"

Ellen and her friends glanced at one another with alarm.

"Edna?" Ellen asked the darkness. "Edna, are you okay?"

"What if it's hurting her?" Tanya murmured. "What do we do? Sue, do you have your holy water?"

Sue fumbled through her purse.

"Jack? Jack! You brought my Jack home to me!"

Ellen turned to her friends. "The man in the road was Jack Jackson? Edna's Jack?"

Sue gawked.

"Maybe they can finally cross over!" Tanya said.

"Edna?" Sue called out. "Are you still here?"

"I'm here with Jack! My sweet, darling Jack! Oh, how I've missed you! Where have you been? Looking for me? But I've been looking for you!"

"Edna?" Ellen said. "It's time for you and Jack to move on, okay? You don't need to stay here any longer."

"Cross over into the light!" Tanya said.

"May the two of you find eternal peace!" Sue added.

The light on the front desk flickered and burnt out. Ellen and her friends stood in the quiet darkness, listening.

Then Ellen said, "Edna? You there?"

Not five feet away, a luminous young couple appeared. The man looked tall and thin and haggard, but he was smiling now as he held a young pregnant woman in his arms.

Overcome by shock at the sight of the ghosts so near her, Ellen couldn't speak.

"You found each other," Sue whispered. "Now you can move on."

The ghost of Edna smiled at them before the luminous couple disappeared.

Ellen, Sue, and Tanya stood silently in awe for a full minute before Ellen finally said, "Edna? Are you still here?"

She and her friends stood there, holding their breath. The silence was reassuring.

Then Tanya headed toward the elevator, pulling her bag behind her. Sue and Ellen followed.

Once inside the elevator, Tanya, her eyes full of tears, sighed. "I hope they moved on."

"Me, too," Sue said, wiping a tear from her cheek.

Ellen smiled at her friends, finally allowing her tears to fall. "Me, three."

Once Ellen had allowed her tears to fall, she couldn't make them stop, especially once she was alone in her room. As she changed into her pajamas, she cried. Even as she brushed her teeth and washed her face, she cried. After climbing into bed beneath the fresh, clean linens and turning off the lamp beside her, she cried and cried and cried.

She wasn't thinking of Edna and Jack. She was thinking of Paul.

CHAPTER EIGHTEEN

An Unexpected Find

Tuesday morning, Ellen slept in and spent the day alone in her hotel room. Despite her recent success in Boulder City, she was feeling melancholy. Both the mayor and Chief Needham had called her to personally thank her for her role in healing their town. She should be on Cloud Nine, not moping around her room.

Part of her mood came from the realization that she had never properly mourned the loss of Paul. And the other part came from the guilt she felt over falling in love with Brian.

She had just put a tray of empty lunch dishes outside her door when her phone rang. It was Brian calling.

"Hi, there," she said.

"Hi, Ellen. You don't sound well. Are you okay?"

"Just tired."

"Hey, I wanted to let you know how sorry I am for being a presumptuous ass. I've decided to put the old Boulder City Hospital property back on the market."

"What?"

"You don't sound happy. I thought you didn't want it."

"I *do* want it," she said. "I just felt weird about receiving it as a gift."

"Because you thought there'd be strings? I thought you knew me better than that."

"Not strings, exactly. It's hard to explain."

"You've told me I'm a pretty good listener."

"You're an excellent listener."

"So, let me listen. Explain. What was weird about accepting my gift? Help me to understand, so I don't make the same mistake in the future."

She was relieved that he still felt like they had a future. "I spent over thirty years in a relationship where I had less control than I should have had over my life—up until the last few years."

"I didn't know that about you. You don't seem like the kind of woman who could be controlled by anyone."

"It wasn't Paul's fault. It was mine. He was the primary breadwinner, so I deferred to his authority. I felt like his financial contribution to our household gave him more say than me in our decisions about what to do with our money."

She waited for Brian to say something, and when he didn't, she asked, "Are you still there?"

"Yes. I'm listening. I can understand why you felt that way, but it's too bad."

"I know. Once Tanya and Sue and I hit it big with the oil well, I felt liberated. I finally had the power and control in my marriage, and I began making decisions without even consulting Paul. I soon realized the faultiness in my mindset about the relationship between money and power in a partnership."

"So how does this relate to my gift? Do you think I'm trying to have power over you?"

"No. But I see myself giving up my power. It's nothing Paul did to me. And it's nothing you're doing to me. It's me doing it to myself. I feel like I have more control over my life when I pay for things."

"You let me give you the Raven and Rose."

"I earned it. That's different."

"You more than earned it. In fact, I feel I still owe you a debt. Maybe that's why I keep wanting to give you extravagant gifts."

Ellen smiled. "You don't owe me. But you sound like me. I think I felt that way about Paul. I think I felt like I owed him for being the financial support for our family. My teaching salary was supplemental. We couldn't have lived the kind of life we lived on my salary. So, I did extra chores and did most of the cooking and tried to pay him back by being domestic, even though I worked, too."

"I get it."

"How would you feel about selling the property to me?"

Brian chuckled. "I was hoping to make a profit. Now that you averted the crisis and got rid of the flu and the ghosts, the value should be going back up."

"I'm happy to pay market value. It's only fair."

Brian laughed again. "Hmm. You sure are an interesting cookie."

A few hours later, Ellen asked Kirk to drive her to the property, so she could have a look around in the daytime. She took her sketch pad along, thinking she might like to draw the view of Lake Mead.

"Do you want me to go with you?" Kirk asked once he'd parked at the curb of the estate and opened the back door for her.

She hesitated. Although she felt nervous about revisiting a place that had emblazoned a horrific image in her mind that would likely haunt her for years to come, she'd wanted to be alone; otherwise, she would have invited Sue and Tanya to join her.

"No, thanks," she said. "I'd like to stay for a while. Should I call you when I'm ready?"

"I have nowhere else to be. I'll just wait here. I have a few phone calls I need to make, anyway."

"Thank you, Kirk."

With her sketch pad in hand, she made her way up the hill.

Following the perimeter of the fence, she gazed out over the lake to the east and felt lighter. What was it about seeing a large body of water that engendered peace? She breathed in the fresh, warm air and began to hum.

When she reached the gap in the fence, the memories from her first visit to the property sent a chill down her spine. She gazed up at the concrete steps, paralyzed. She reminded herself that the crime scene had been cleared before the property had been sold. There wouldn't be a body at the top of the hill. There wouldn't be a message written in blood. It would be a clean cement slab, just waiting to have the original building restored on its foundation.

She took a deep breath and headed up the steps.

She hadn't expected to be trembling quite so much, but when she finally reached the top and looked around in the afternoon sun, with the willow swaying in the light breeze and the cement slab sparkling in the sunlight, she felt at ease. To prove to herself that she wasn't a coward, she walked across the gravel, past the mounds of bricks and roof tiles, onto the cement slab, and directly onto the spot where the body had been found.

"See?" she whispered. "It's fine. Nothing has power over you, Ellen. You are in charge of your own destiny."

Even in the sunshine, the city of Las Vegas to the west shimmered and glowed with activity; whereas, Lake Mead, to the east, was like a still and quiet portrait, waiting to be painted. The contrast between the two views was incredible, but both showed what human ingenuity could create from a wasteland.

Ellen found a spot on the edge of the cement foundation where she could sit comfortably with her legs hanging over the side and her feet propped on gravel. She opened her sketch pad and gazed at the lake. Copper hills provided a contrasting backdrop to the dark blue water. The water was like a thick sheet of rich blue paint, except for the small sandy-colored rock formations that reached the surface, providing a spot for resting birds. Ellen put her pencil to work, trying to capture the pastoral majesty that had washed her with peace and tranquility. She spent a good hour creating a landscape she was proud of. Maybe she would use the sketch to create a painting, or maybe she would go over it with charcoal.

As she mulled over what to do with her sketch, she heard an owl hooting from a clump of mesquites to her right. From where she sat, she studied the branches, searching for it.

"There you are," she whispered.

She turned the page in her sketch pad and began to draw the owl.

It had been surprising for her to see an owl in a mesquite, because of the thorns. She wouldn't have expected any bird, much less an owl, to be resting in such an inhospitable tree. Growing up in Texas, she'd always thought mesquites to be ugly, scraggily things; but this clump of trees was full of feathery leaves and soft, yellow blooms. The bird was a great horned owl, with huge yellow eyes, as bright as a cat's, staring down at her. Tufts of feathers set high on its head, resembling horns. Its feathers were brown, with dark brown spots, except for those at the throat, which were white.

Its hoot sounded like a direct question to Ellen: "You awake? Me tooooo. You awake? Me tooooo."

Ellen looked down at her sketch and gasped.

She hadn't been drawing the owl in the mesquite. She'd been drawing the original Boulder City Hospital, which she'd only seen once, on the internet. How was that possible?

Then something else caught her eye. To the right of the building, beneath where she'd drawn the clump of mesquite trees, she'd drawn an X.

She jumped to her feet and paced nervously, wondering if she should flee for the limo or stay put. The eerie sketch reminded her of a paranormal investigation in Tulsa, when Miss Margaret Myrtle had drawn a building on fire and countless black bodies burning, along with the words: *We are here.*

Had Ellen been used as a medium by a ghost with a message? And did that ghost want her to look for something in the ground beneath the mesquite trees?

With her sketch book in hand, she hastened down the concrete steps, through the gap in the fence, along its perimeter, and down the grassy hill toward the limo.

Kirk jumped from the front seat and cried, "What's happened? Are you okay?"

"I'm okay," she said, panting, as she reached him. "Just excited. Can we go back to the hotel and pick up Tanya and Sue?"

"Of course." He opened the back door.

As soon as she was strapped in, Ellen created a group text with Sue and Tanya and wrote: *You won't believe what just happened. Meet me in the hotel lobby. Our work here isn't done.*

In a second text, she wrote: *Wear comfortable shoes.*

She received a text from Sue: *Spill, girlfriend.*

I'm almost there. I'll explain in person.

I wasn't planning on getting dressed today, Sue replied.

Well, get your butt dressed! Ellen texted back.

A few minutes later, Kirk pulled up in front of the hotel.

"I might be a while," Ellen said. "Sue still hasn't gotten dressed."

"No problem, ma'am."

"Would you mind using your phone to locate the nearest hardware store? We'll need to buy a shovel and probably a pair of gloves."

"Would you like me to pick those items up for you now?" he asked.

"Oh, would you?"

"Yes, ma'am."

"Thank you so much! Will you text me when you've returned?"

"It would be my pleasure."

Ellen hastened into the hotel lobby, where Tanya was already seated with a warm cup of tea in front of the empty fireplace.

"Did you get my text?" Ellen asked.

"No. Why? Has something happened?"

Ellen told her friend about the drawing she'd done while looking at the owl. "It was like what happened to Miss Myrtle in Tulsa. And look at this X."

"What? That's bizarre. You aren't playing a prank on me, are you?"

"Tanya, I'm serious. I'm either crazy or something used me as a medium."

"You think something's buried there, where the X is?" Tanya asked.

"I don't know, but Kirk just went to buy me a shovel and a pair of gloves."

Twenty minutes later, Ellen struck the blade of the shovel against the rocky ground beneath the mesquites on the old Boulder City Hospital property. Shocked that the owl hadn't moved, she warned her friends not to frighten it away by speaking loudly.

"I doubt it will come to that," Sue whispered. "You're making enough noise on your own."

Sue was right. The ground was as rocky as the soil in San Antonio but drier, despite the deluge that had fallen a week ago from the storm that had nearly killed them. She used her foot to push the head of the shovel into the ground. And, when that didn't work, she stepped on it, using her weight, until the blade finally broke the surface.

"The view up here is truly breathtaking," Sue said as she gazed to the east.

"I'm glad you're enjoying it." Ellen grunted as she continued to use her body weight to make progress. "These rocks are huge—bigger than what we dig up in our Texas gardens."

"Maybe we should go out for ice cream after this," Sue said. "I'm melting in this heat."

"Let me have a turn." Tanya reached for the shovel.

For the next half hour, Tanya and Ellen took turns digging, while Sue supervised. Tanya was the one digging when the head of the shovel hit against something that made a *clap*.

"That doesn't sound like rock," Sue said. "Thank goodness, because my feet are killing me."

Ellen and Tanya knelt on the ground and used their hands to dig in the two-foot hole around what appeared to be a metal box. Ellen grabbed the shovel and used the blade to loosen the box from the dry, hard dirt.

Tanya lifted the box into her hands and wiped dirt from the top of it. "It's an old first aid kit."

"Open it," Ellen said.

"The lid's stuck," Tanya said.

Sue put her hands on her hips. "Why don't we take it back with us and open it in the limo, where we can sit down and have a drink?"

Ellen grabbed the shovel and slammed the head against the box.

The rusty hinges disintegrated. Ellen used her fingernails to pry the lid open.

Inside, she found a glass jar with a yellowed piece of paper folded inside of it.

When Ellen couldn't get the lid of the jar opened, she passed it to Tanya, who tried and then passed it to Sue. None of them could open it.

Defeated, they carried the box, shovel, gloves, and jar back to the limo to solicit help from Kirk. Sue climbed into the back of the car to rest her feet and drink some water while Ellen and Tanya beat the dirt from their hands and clothes. Standing beside Ellen, Kirk strained to open the jar.

"You did it!" Ellen cried.

She took the yellowed paper from inside of the jar and carefully unfolded it.

CHAPTER NINETEEN

Messages from Beyond

"What's it say?" Tanya asked.

Ellen squinted at the writing on the fragile sheet of paper she had taken from the jar.

"We may need to analyze this with a magnifying glass," she said. "The writing is difficult to make out."

"Let me see it." Tanya took the paper from Ellen. "It's a list of names. I recognize some of them from the bureau records."

"Can I have a look?" Sue asked from inside the limo. "I've always been told I have eagle eyes."

"You wear readers," Ellen complained.

"Perception is more than good vision," she said. "It also has to do with being able to understand the patterns. Besides, I have a magnifying glass in my purse."

"You do?" Ellen leaned over to look at Sue. "Whatever for?"

"Moments like this, of course. Now climb inside and close the door, so Kirk can get the air going."

Ellen and Tanya climbed into the back of the limo as Sue opened her keychain to reveal a magnifying glass the size of a quarter.

"May I?" Ellen asked.

Begrudgingly, Sue handed over her keys, and Ellen held the magnifying glass up to the page.

Aloud, Ellen read the words, handwritten in black ink, as she was able to make them out: "'I, Dr. Anthony Bridgewater,'" Ellen looked up. "Oh, my gosh! This is a letter from Dr. Bridgewater!"

"Don't stop now!" Sue prodded. "Read what it says!"

Ellen read: "'I, Dr. Anthony Bridgewater, did as I was told, but I cannot, in good conscience, leave this hospital without leaving a list for posterity of all those who died of carbon monoxide poisoning while building the Boulder Dam.'"

"Oh my gosh," Ellen murmured. "Oh, my gosh!"

"This is incontrovertible evidence!" Tanya said.

"There's fifty names listed," Ellen said, "which means we missed two."

"We need to call Chief Needham right away," Sue said. "He needs to come to the site and see where we found it, so he doesn't think we're making this up."

"And we need to petition the Bureau of Reclamation to change the monument on the dam from 96 to 146 deaths," Ellen said. "Do you think they'll do it?"

"I sure hope so," Sue said. "I would think they'd take the ghost of the doctor seriously by now. Don't you?"

"And don't forget the death records," Tanya said. "They need to be amended to reflect the truth."

"This is so exciting," Ellen said. "I can't believe the spirit of a doctor from the 1930s was able to communicate this through my drawing."

"Maybe you have a gift, like Miss Myrtle," Tanya said. "You should start bringing your sketch pad with you to our investigations."

Ellen sucked in her lips. That would be a remarkable way to combine her love of art with her calling to help lost souls.

"I think I will," she said with a smile.

As Sue called the chief, Ellen noticed the great horned owl spread its magnificent wings as it sprang over the hilltop and soared into the bright blue sky.

That evening, after washing the desert dirt from her hair and skin, Ellen changed into fresh clothes and met her friends in the lobby before dinner. Sue had heard from several locals at a nearby bakery that the best place to eat in town was the Southwest Diner and that the fish tacos were a local favorite. Kirk was waiting in the limo in front of the hotel.

As they waited for their order at a square table in the quaint diner, Ellen told them that she was buying the old Boulder City Hospital estate from Brian.

"Seriously?" Tanya asked. "Even after what happened there?"

"Seriously," Ellen said. "Think about it. The doctor was trying to get our attention. No one was actually *hurt*."

"What about Hunter Merton?" Sue asked.

"Good point," Tanya said.

"I'm sure it was traumatizing for Hunter," Ellen said. "And that's unfortunate. However, the city is dropping all charges. He can put the whole incident behind him, just as we can."

"So, what are you going to do?" Sue asked. "Are you going to let Brian turn it into another Kennedy School?"

"I'm thinking about it," Ellen said. "It would make a really interesting hotel, especially with those breathtaking views. I think we could honor the history of the Hoover Dam, the Depression, and Boulder City while creating an interesting restaurant, bar, hotel, and museum."

"By *we*, you mean you and Brian?" Tanya asked.

"Not necessarily," Ellen said. "Any chance the two of you would be interested in helping with the renovations?"

"I thought you'd never ask," Sue said. "Ever since you told us that Brian bought the place, I've been researching the original building for ideas."

"You have?" Ellen asked.

"Did you know that the lot was originally *meant* for a hotel?" Sue said.

"No, I didn't," Ellen said.

"Oh, yes," Sue said. "It wasn't until Six Companies realized how impractical it was for workers to travel to Vegas for healthcare that they quickly changed their plans and built a hospital instead."

"Do you think they did it because they recognized the benefit of having doctors under their employ and under their thumbs?" Tanya asked.

"Interesting question," Ellen said. "Did they build the hospital because they were corrupt? Or did they become corrupt because they built the hospital?"

"I guess we'll never know," Tanya said.

"When they first built it, there were only twenty beds," Sue said. "But if we outfit the operating rooms, waiting rooms, and offices, I believe you can rent out thirty or forty rooms."

"The museum would be integrated rather than separate from hotel, right?" Ellen said. "More like Kennedy than the Boulder Dam Hotel?"

"That's what I was thinking," Sue said.

"What about the restaurant?" Tanya asked.

"I've got that covered," Sue said. "The isolation ward. That might even be the name of the bar!"

"What a clever idea, Sue!" Ellen said with a laugh.

Sue shrugged and batted her eyes. "I've been known to come up with one or two."

As the waitress delivered their food, a man in his thirties approached their table and said, "Thank you for saving Boulder City. Would you mind if I asked you a few questions?"

Sue looked over the delicious food they had just been served. Then she put her hands on her hips and turned towards the man.

"Uh-oh," Tanya said.

"If I were you, I'd leave," Ellen told the reporter. "Before you get an earful."

As excited as Ellen had been at dinner over their plans for rebuilding the original hospital and transforming it into a museum, restaurant, and hotel, when she returned to her room and readied for bed, she was overcome by sadness.

Maybe it was the second margarita Sue had convinced her to have with dinner. Alcohol sometimes made her feel blue.

She dug her Kindle from her purse and climbed into bed, hoping to find a good mystery to read, when her phone rang. It was Brian.

"I got your text," he said. "You've had a big day. I want to hear all about it."

She was so unused to having a partner who was interested in hearing about the details of her day, that she replayed everything to Brian with childlike enthusiasm. After she told him what had happened, he told her about a new project he was thinking of acquiring in southern Washington. He told her a bit about its history, which she found fascinating. By the time they hung up, two hours had passed.

The lift in mood from her conversation with Brian dissipated not long after she'd ended their call. She began to dwell on the differences between her relationship with Brian and the thirty years she spent with Paul.

Paul had always done his thing, and she'd always done hers, and they rarely told one another the details. She'd ask, "How was your golf game?" and Paul would either say, "I played well," or "Not so good." That would be the extent of it. And, when she'd return from a trip with the girls, or from an art show, or whatever, sometimes he'd ask, "Did you have a good time?" and sometimes he'd ask nothing at all.

But it hadn't always been that way. While they were dating, she'd learned to play golf and to fish and to play cards and had enjoyed doing those things with him. He occasionally attended an art show or a musical but made little effort to engage in activities that she enjoyed. At some point, after they were married, she stopped trying altogether. For the past fifteen years, the only glue holding them together came from their children and their memories together.

So why did she feel this horrible pain in the pit of her stomach over the loss of Paul? Why couldn't she allow herself to let go and move on, wholly and completely?

Was it because she felt guilty that things hadn't been better, and that he had died before she had had a chance to turn things around?

Or was it that, despite their independent lives, they had come to depend on one another in a way that could never be replaced, not even by Brian?

Ellen felt restless and decided to go downstairs to the vending machine for a snack. There were people visiting in the lobby, but she avoided them, lest they accost her, as other reporters and paranormal investigators had been doing all week. She found the vending machine not far from the elevator and looked over her options. She was startled by a voice near her ear.

"Hello, dear."

It was the lobby ghost.

"Edna? I thought you crossed over with Jack!" Ellen cried, and then, not wanting to draw the attention of anyone, she added, "Why are you still here?"

"I did crossover, Ellen. Not many people can go back and forth, but I can. I think it's because I'm with-child. Or maybe it's because I'm a night person. At any rate, I just dropped in to give you a message from Paul."

Ellen froze. Her mouth was suddenly dry, and her head became dizzy. She grabbed ahold of the vending machine, to keep from stumbling to the floor.

Was she imagining this? Or was it real? Was she awake? Or would she be opening her eyes any moment, only to realize she'd been dreaming?

"Paul asked me to tell you that everything is okay."

With barely enough breath or energy to utter the word, Ellen rasped, "What?"

"Paul said to tell you that everything is okay. You needn't worry anymore."

"Ellen?"

Ellen turned to see Sue approaching from the elevator.

"Ellen, are you okay? You don't look well."

"I need to sit down," Ellen said. "Not here. Let's go back upstairs."

"Okay, sure. I just want to get a pack of Ding Dongs first. Can you wait a minute?"

Ellen nodded, still leaning on the machine and trying to catch her breath.

"Did something happen?" Sue asked as she punched in the number for the Ding Dongs.

"Edna…she can go back and forth."

"She came back?"

Ellen nodded. "You still with us, Edna?"

Ellen and Sue waited in silence but heard nothing more.

"What did she say to you?" Sue asked as she pulled her pack of Ding Dongs from the machine.

"She said that…" Ellen broke into tears.

Sue helped Ellen back into the elevator.

"There, there," Sue said. "Take your time. Remember to breathe."

"Edna said that she had a message from Paul," Ellen finally managed to say as they rode the elevator up to their floor.

"Oh my God! *Your* Paul?"

"What other Paul would it be?"

"What was the message?"

"Everything will be okay. I needn't worry anymore."

Ellen sobbed as a flood of emotion washed over her and through her and out of her. Sue helped her from the elevator and back to her room.

Tanya poked her head out from her hotel room and asked, "What's going on? Ellen, what happened?"

Sue told her about Edna's message from Paul.

"You're so lucky!" Tanya said. "Few people ever get to hear from their loved ones once they've passed."

"I wish I could talk to him one more time," Ellen said from where she stood in the hall outside her hotel room. "I can't tell you how many times I've considered using the Ouija Board or the pendulum and the electromagnetic pump to make contact with him."

"Why haven't you?" Sue asked.

"Because I'm sure he's in a good place, and I don't want him to get stuck here because of me. I want him to be at peace."

"Why would he tell you that you needn't worry?" Tanya asked. "Have you been worrying about something?"

"About him. I've been worried about hurting him." Ellen leaned her back against her door and slid all the way down to the floor as she spoke through her tears. She hugged her knees. "I don't want him to think I'm replacing him. I need him to know that, despite the flaws in our marriage, I loved him with all my heart. What if he doesn't know that? What if he thinks I'm happier and better off with Brian?"

"Are you happier and better off with Brian?" Sue asked.

Ellen covered her face with her hands and wept.

"Paul obviously wants you to be at peace with this," Tanya said. "If he went to the trouble to ask Edna to give you the message that everything is okay and that you needn't worry, he must want you to be happy."

"Paul knows that you loved him," Sue said. "You spent over thirty years together, you raised a family together. He knows."

Ellen shook as she was wracked with sobs. Tanya came from her room and sat on the floor beside Ellen. Even Sue, who rarely got down on the floor for any reason, did the same. Her best friends patted her shoulders and told her it would be okay.

Sue opened her pack of Ding Dongs and said, "Anybody want one?"

Ellen smiled. Then she giggled. Tanya giggled, too.

"So much for counting calories," Ellen said.

"Just while we're traveling," Sue assured her. "I'll start dieting when we get home."

"Well, then, you better enjoy those Ding Dongs while you can," Ellen said as she wiped the tears from her eyes. "Because I booked us a flight home tomorrow."

CHAPTER TWENTY

Return to Boulder City

Two months later, on Halloween, Ellen, Sue, and Tanya returned to Boulder City for a ground-breaking ceremony on the lot where the Boulder City Hospital Hotel would soon be built. Brian, Kiernan, Chief Needham, and a crowd of reporters and citizens joined them as Ellen dedicated the hotel to the memory of the fifty men who died of carbon monoxide poisoning while building Hoover Dam. Many of the citizens present were descendants of those men whose sacrifice had not been properly recorded.

Holding a microphone in one hand and a shovel in the other, Ellen stood on the hilltop in the afternoon sun with Sue, Tanya, and Brian at her side. She addressed the crowd and smiled at their cameras and videorecorders:

"After we discovered a letter buried on these grounds from physician Anthony Bridgewater confessing to the doctoring of death records of fifty men in the early 1930s, due to pressure by Six Companies to avoid having to pay families workmen's compensation, we petitioned the Bureau of Reclamation to alter the Hoover Dam Memorial to reflect the fact that 146, not 96, men died to make the desert bloom. The Bureau refused. They said the memorial was a historical work of art that could not be changed. They also did not find the letter we discovered or the Phantom Flu and related hauntings to be compelling enough. The bureau did, however, agree to add a note in the records acknowledging that the official count of industrial deaths during the dam's construction could be inaccurate. It's not what we were hoping for, but it's something."

Ellen paused while the crowd applauded—though not very enthusiastically.

"But we can do better than that," she assured them. "Our team of architects and interior designers has put together a plan that will create fifty rooms in the forthcoming Boulder City Hospital Hotel—each one dedicated to the memory of one of the fifty men who were unjustly treated."

This time the applause exploded. Ellen smiled at the crowd, encouraged by their energy.

"My team and I have been conducting research on these workers— talking to descendants and looking at photographs, diaries, and historical documents that have been passed down within families. We're doing our due diligence to make sure the sacrifice of these fifty men in the construction of the dam is honored and never forgotten."

The crowd erupted once more.

"The hotel will be a monument to those fifty men, but it will also provide insight to its visitors of what it was like to be an American during the Depression in Boulder City. My team and I have designed the restaurant and bar with materials and structures reminiscent of the Ragtown camps that were first built on Hemenway Wash."

She stuck the blade of the shovel into the hard earth. "Today we break ground and begin our journey in honoring our past."

After her speech, Ellen answered questions from reporters and citizens of Boulder City about the project and about the role she played in healing the city from the Phantom Flu. Sue helped her to answer some of the questions. Even Tanya said a few words.

"What's next?" one reporter asked. "Where will Ghost Healers, Inc, go from here?"

Ellen glanced at Sue and Tanya.

Sue took the microphone. "As much as we enjoy the attention, we're not at liberty to say. We work best when we aren't being hounded by reporters and other paranormal investigators—no offense."

Later, when Ellen, Sue, and Tanya were in the back of a limo rental with Brian on their way to the Boulder Dam Hotel, Tanya said, "What do you think happened to the ghost of Ferris Kahn? Do you think it returned to Hoover Dam?"

"Probably," Ellen said, "but the only way to know for sure is to return to the dam to conduct a séance."

Sue lifted her chin. "That sounds like the perfect way to spend Halloween! Brian, do you think Kiernan's son can get us in?"

"I can give him a call and find out."

That evening, after beer and burgers at the Dillinger, Kirk drove the group to meet Matt at the dam. While Kirk waited in the Arizona visitor's parking lot in the limo, Matt escorted Ellen, Brian, Sue, and Tanya in the Arizona elevator down to the visitor's gallery. From there, they trekked through the winding tunnels to the old viewing area, where, two months ago, the window between the observation room and the penstock had cracked as the word "Help" had formed in the condensation on the pane.

"You know how to find your way back?" Matt asked Brian.

"Sure, man. Thanks."

"Don't break nothing," Matt said. "I don't want to lose my job."

Brian glanced at Ellen. "I can't make any promises."

"You're killing me, man."

"We promise not to break a dam thing," Sue said. "But we aren't responsible for the actions of ghosts."

"Fair enough," Matt said. "Happy Halloween."

"Happy Halloween," they called back to him as he left them alone in the room.

"Are we really going to do this?" Brian asked Ellen and her friends.

"What, are you scared?" Sue taunted him.

"Dam right. You should be, too."

"Honestly, we are," Tanya said.

"Then why do you do it?" Brian wanted to know.

"Two reasons," Ellen said. "One is because we feel called to help lost souls."

Brian nodded. "What's the other reason?"

"Because it's dam thrilling!" Sue said, so loudly that her voice echoed through the old diversion tunnel on the other side of the glass.

Ellen grabbed her notebook to take some baseline readings as Tanya called out the temperature and Sue reported her EMF readings. Then they made a circle of salt around themselves and sat in the center with the Ouija Board, a candle, and half-eaten brownie that Sue ordered for dessert but couldn't finish.

Although they had left their full-spectrum cameras and electromagnetic pump behind, Ellen turned on her handheld audio recorder, while Tanya adjusted her phone on a very small portable stand and hit the record button.

"Just promise me one thing before we get started," Sue said as they leaned over the board and placed their fingertips on the planchette.

"What?" Tanya asked.

"If Ferris Kahn appears and scares us half to death, don't run off without helping me up first. I don't want to be left behind in this dam place."

Tanya rolled her eyes. Ellen and Brian exchanged grins.

"Are we ready to begin?' Ellen asked.

The others nodded and settled themselves as Ellen took a deep breath.

"Oh, spirits of the other realm," Ellen began, "we mean you no harm. We come in peace, looking for Ferris Kahn. Ferris, are you here?"

They sat in silence with only the light of the candle and a dim fluorescent light in the diversion tunnel illuminating the room.

When nothing happened, Ellen said, "Spirits of the other realm, we mean no harm. We're looking for Ferris Kahn. Are you here? If so, please give us a sign."

The candle blew out.

Ellen squinted at the ceiling, looking for a vent that might have blown air and extinguished the candle, but she saw nothing but the tiles of a drop ceiling.

"Ferris Kahn," Sue began. "Are you here?"

The planchette moved to YES.

"Is this Ferris?" Tanya asked.

YES.

"When were you born?" Ellen asked, to test the spirit, just in case it was lying.

"1-8-8-2."

"What month?" Tanya asked.

"M-A-Y."

"That's right," Sue said, "according to his obituary."

Brian's mouth fell open.

"When did you die?" Ellen asked.

"1-9-5-8."

"How did you die?" Tanya asked.

"H-E-A-R-T-A-T-T-A-C-K."

"Right again," Sue whispered.

"This is incredible," Brian whispered.

"Why are you here?" Ellen asked, "Why haven't you moved on to the other side?"

"H-E-L-L."

"You're in hell?" Tanya asked.

"YES."

"But, if you're in hell," Sue began, "how can you be here?"

"S-A-M-E."

"Same?" Brian read. "Is Hoover Dam hell?"

"NO."

The planchette circled around the board and spelled: "S-T-A-T-E."

"State," Tanya read with a frown.

The planchette continued, "N-O-T-P-L-A-C-E."

"Oh," Ellen said.

Together, she and Brian said, "Hell is a state, not a place."

Sue cleared her voice. "Maybe if you forgive yourself, you can move on."

They sat in the silence waiting.

"Ferris Kahn? Are you still there?" Sue asked.

"YES."

She said again, "Maybe if you forgive yourself, you can move on."

"C-A-N-T."

"I wonder if that means he can't forgive himself or can't move on, even if he does forgive himself," Brian wondered out loud.

The planchette moved to the number 1.

"He can't forgive himself," Ellen said. "I don't blame him. What he did was selfish and unfair."

"It was," Tanya agreed.

"But he didn't kill anybody," Sue said. "He just made a doctor lie about the cause of death."

"An injustice to the memory of those men and to their families," Ellen said.

"He cheated families out of workmen's comp during a time when every penny counted," Brian said.

"He lied, cheated, and stole from the poor," Tanya said.

"But those aren't unforgiveable acts," Sue said. "Wouldn't you agree? His soul has been stuck here, tormented in a state of hell since 1958. How long should he have to pay for his greed and selfishness. Forever?"

Ellen said, "No," as the planchette moved to "YES."

"Not forever," Tanya said. "Everyone deserves a chance at redemption, no matter how vile the crime."

"Even murder?" Sue asked.

"Yes," Tanya said.

"I agree," Ellen said.

"So do I," Brian said. "Forgive yourself, man."

Ellen took a deep breath. "Ferris Kahn, I'm no priest, but I believe you have absolved yourself of sin. Let yourself cross to the other side. Forgive yourself and move on."

Suddenly the plastic planchette cracked beneath their fingertips as a buzzing sound, like a swarm of bees, echoed in the diversion tunnel. Ellen climbed to her feet to look at the penstock through the windowpane, worried something bad was about to happen. What if Ferris was angry and wished to drown them?

The fluorescent light in the diversion tunnel flickered and buzzed until it went completely out, leaving Ellen and her friends in total darkness.

Ellen scrambled for her phone, and once she turned on the flashlight app, she shined it all around the room, making sure her friends were okay.

Everyone was fine, as they, too, shined their lights to stave off the darkness.

Ellen's light fell upon the window that looked out over the diversion tunnel. She was shocked by the word written there in a thin layer of dust: Goodbye.

Had Ferris Kahn moved on? Or had he simply left, tired of their questions?

Ellen supposed they would never know.

Later, while they were riding in the limo on their way to the Boulder Dam Hotel, Brian told Ellen how proud he was of her and her friends and what they had accomplished, not just for the city, but for the sake of history.

"You really shined today at that ground-breaking ceremony," he added.

"Thanks," she said, unable to stop from beaming.

Sue said, "I can't tell you how close I came to telling those reporters about our next project."

"What next project?" Ellen asked.

Tanya wrinkled her nose. "What are you talking about, Sue?"

"I received an interesting email through my blog from a woman in Glacier County, Montana. I really think that the ghost of Blackfeet Nation should be the focus of our next investigation."

THE END

Thank you for reading my story. I hope you enjoyed it! If you did, please consider leaving a review. Reviews help other readers to discover my books, which helps me.

Please enjoy the first chapter of the next book in the series, *The Ghost of Blackfeet Nation.*

CHAPTER ONE:

A Midnight Emergency

"Did I wake you?" Tanya asked Ellen over the phone.

Ellen sat up in her recliner—what used to be *Paul's* recliner—and paused the Netflix show she was watching. "I'm a night owl, remember? Everything okay?"

Tanya sounded frantic. "No. Dave's out of town. I called Sue, and she's on the way over, but now I'm worried she'll use her gun."

Ellen jumped to her feet. "Tanya? What's going on? Why would Sue use a gun?"

"Can I explain when you get here?" Tanya said. "I need you on my side."

"Do I need a bra for this?" Ellen was serious. Putting one on would slow her down.

"No. Just hurry."

Ellen ended the call, turned off the television, and slipped on her shoes, all the while wondering what could possibly be wrong at Tanya's house.

When Ellen arrived, she pulled up near the curb behind Sue's Porsche Taycan and scrambled to the front door.

Tanya opened it immediately. Her blonde hair was pulled back into a ponytail, and her blue eyes were red, as though she'd been crying. "It's out back."

"What is?" Ellen asked as she followed Tanya through the house. "Do I need a weapon?"

"God, no. It's just an armadillo."

Ellen grabbed Tanya's hand and turned her around to face her. "Wait a minute. Did you get me all worked up over an armadillo?"

Tears filled Tanya's eyes. "I think it's dying, and it's all my fault."

Ellen followed Tanya through the back door to the yard outside, where Sue was standing over a small cage containing an armadillo lying on its side.

"Is it still breathing?" Tanya asked Sue.

"Barely," she said as she pushed her brown bangs from her eyes. "You sure you don't want me to put it out of its misery?"

"Can someone explain to me what's going on?" Ellen insisted.

Through her tears, Tanya said, "Dave set out this trap, because something's been digging up my garden. Then he went out of town on Friday, and I forgot all about it, until this evening. This poor animal has been trapped inside that cage without food or water in this summer heat for maybe three days, and we need to save it. I tried putting water in there, but he didn't move."

"What's the plan?" Ellen asked.

"There's a place I know where we could release it. I was hoping one of you would drive, since I don't like driving at night."

Sue put her hands on her wide hips. "I could have helped you with that. You didn't need to drag Ellen here, too."

Tanya glanced nervously at Ellen.

"I don't mind," Ellen said. "I'll grab the cage. Sue better drive."

"Oh, that's right," Sue said. "I forgot about your new Jag."

Ellen had recently splurged on a shiny blue Jaguar, to mark the beginning of a new chapter in her life. It had been meant as a pick-me-up, but she should have known that material things, no matter how sexy and exciting, can only do so much.

"My trunk would be too hot," Ellen said. "Unless you don't mind sitting with the cage in the backseat."

Sue laughed. "I think I'd rather have raw eggs thrown at me."

Ellen and Tanya laughed as Ellen said, "We could arrange for that, I suppose."

"Maybe another time," Sue said. "Come on. I'll drive."

After they were on the road, Ellen asked from the back, "So, where is this place, Tanya?"

"Not too far," Tanya said from the passenger's seat. "It's that new area under development just north of us."

Sue blanched. "Won't there be tractors and other equipment tearing up the land? I wouldn't think that would be safe for the critter, but I'm no expert."

"Are you talking about where they're building that new strip mall right off of 281?" Ellen asked.

Tanya glanced back. "Yeah. Why?"

"Isn't it too close to the highway?" Ellen pointed out.

"I'm beginning to doubt that you care about that poor creature," Sue teased.

Tanya was soon in tears again. "What do we do, guys?"

"I vote for McAllister Park," Ellen said.

"That's a good idea." Tanya wiped her eyes with her sleeve. "Sorry, I'm just not thinking straight."

Sue did a U-turn and headed for the park. Fifteen minutes later, they stood beneath a tree canopy staring at the cage on the ground. The SUV was parked on the side of the road about fifty yards away. The park was quiet and empty. Ellen hoped the animal was still alive.

"I wish I had gloves," Tanya said as she reached out with a shaky hand. "I'm scared to touch it."

Sue rolled her eyes. "I'll do it."

She lifted the door to the cage and then uttered a hysterical cry as the armadillo jumped to its feet and scrambled past her and into the woods. Sue lost her balance and fell back onto the dirt.

Tanya leaned over her. "Are you okay?"

Sue busted out laughing. "That scared the heck out of me!"

Once she'd recovered from the shock, Ellen laughed, too, and offered Sue a hand. "Do armadillos play dead?"

"I guess so," Tanya said. "What a relief! I can't thank you guys enough! I'm sorry to have dragged you out here in the middle of the night. I owe you, big time."

"I know how you can thank me." Sue wiped the dirt and dried leaves from the back of her capri pants. "Why don't we grab a lemon loaf and a latte at Starbucks while you hear me out?"

Ellen followed her friends to the Taycan. "I hope you mean to drive through, because I'm not wearing a bra."

"Just carry your purse in front of you," Sue said.

Sue had to drive a bit further to find a Starbucks with a café that was open twenty-four hours, but she managed, and once they were sitting around a table with their lattes and cakes, she said, "Promise me that you'll keep an open mind."

Ellen and Tanya glanced at one another.

"I know you two wanted to pass on the project at Blackfeet Nation," Sue began, "but hear me out."

Ellen sighed. They'd already been over this a million times.

"Montana's too far," Tanya said.

"I get that you guys aren't interested in a vacation home near Glacier National Park—though it's still beyond me why. It's the crown of the continent, and the most beautiful place in America."

"I don't want to fly any more often than is necessary," Tanya reminded her. "Not after that crash landing in Brian's plane. We could have *died*."

Sue took a sip of her latte. "I'm not going to say all the things I've already said to try to change your mind—like the fact that the Blackfeet are practically giving the house away, along with the one hundred acres it sits on, or the fact that it's located right where the majestic Rocky Mountains meet the sweeping grassy plains, or the fact that the train is roomy and will boast amazing views along the way."

Tanya groaned as she took a bite of her lemon loaf.

For someone who wasn't going to say all the things she'd already said, Sue was saying quite a lot, Ellen thought as she sipped her latte.

"However," Sue paused dramatically. "I want the house for myself, and I'm asking you, begging you, as my dearest friends, to help me with the paranormal investigation. I'll take care of all the renovations. I'll pay for all of our expenses while we're there. And I'll make the three-day train ride worth your while."

Ellen lifted her brows. "How do you intend to do that?"

"I don't know yet, but I'll think of something."

Ellen and Tanya glanced dubiously at one another again, but Ellen was feeling less reluctant than she'd felt in the past. An entire year had passed since the Boulder City Hospital Hotel and Museum had been completed, and she was itching for another adventure.

A lot had happened since then. Ellen and Brian had broken up, Sue's mother Jan had passed away, and Tanya had fostered a five and six-year-old brother and sister, who'd just been returned to their mother upon her release from prison. All three of their hearts had been broken.

"I wasn't going to play the grief card," Sue said with tears in her eyes, "but I need to get away."

Ellen bit her bottom lip, recalling how she had felt in the wake of Paul's death. She understood all too well.

"I need to get away from San Antonio," Sue said, breaking down. "I need a distraction."

Tanya reached across the table to squeeze Sue's hand. "I still miss my mother, but it does get easier."

Ellen felt a tinge of guilt for not thinking of her own mother. She'd thought only of Paul.

"At least we finally found someone to take over at the Gold House," Sue said. "That was a nightmare, wasn't it?"

"I'll go with you," Ellen blurted out. "I'll help you with the investigation, and, if you want, the renovation, too."

Sue's brows shot up. "Really? Does that mean you want to go in with me?"

"I don't know yet," Ellen said. "I'll need to see the house and the property first."

"Of course."

They turned to Tanya, who said, "Thanks a lot for throwing me under the bus, Ellen."

"Not under the bus," she said. "On the *train.* Come on. I'm anxious to see how Sue plans to make it worth our while."

Sue lifted her brows. "I guess you're going to hold me to it, even in my grief."

Tanya shook her head. "She's just teasing. Your company is enough to make it worth our while. Wouldn't you agree, Ellen?"

Ellen cocked her head to the side. "Let me get back to you on that."

Sue lobbed a piece of her lemon loaf at Ellen's face. The cake bounced off Ellen's nose and onto the floor.

"Darn," Sue said. "I wanted that bite. Thanks for getting me all riled up."

The three friends laughed.

A week later, in mid-July, as Ellen boarded the train with her friends, she felt a sense of panic. She had forgotten to call her kids to let them know that she was leaving town. When Paul was still alive, she hadn't felt it was necessary to tell her kids about her every move. It had been the same while she was dating Brian. But now there was no one waiting for her at home. If something were to happen to her and to her friends—if the train crashed and killed them—there would be no one alive who'd be aware of her absence for however long it would take the police to notify the family.

As she made her way to her seat, she chastised herself for being silly. Nothing was going to happen to them; yet it felt strange that there was no one waiting for her to check in, to touch base, to hear about her day.

Once she was settled next to Tanya in her seat with Sue sitting across the aisle from her, Ellen took out her phone and texted her kids. The panic in her chest lessened.

Then Sue asked, "Do they serve margaritas on this train?"

Ellen smiled. "I believe they do."

Sue's big brown eyes brightened.

"This is better than the sleeper room, don't you think?" Tanya asked. "These seats go all the way back, and no one has to sleep on top."

"From what I've heard, Ellen likes being on top," Sue teased.

"I plan to spend most of the trip in the sightseer lounge anyway," Ellen said, ignoring her friend's crass remark.

"Did you remember to download the national park podcast I told you about?" Sue asked.

"I'll do that now," Ellen said.

Ellen thought of Brian. They'd parted ways six months ago at a national park. She hoped that fact wouldn't ruin all national parks for her.

No. She wouldn't let it, she thought, as tears sprang to her eyes.

Once the train was underway, Tanya leaned forward and asked Sue, "So, what do you know about this property, anyway?"

"It's called Talks to Buffalo Lodge. It's a two-story ranch that was built in 1890 and has been haunted since the 1940s, if not earlier," Sue said. "And it's been vacant since the seventies."

"Since the seventies? No wonder the Blackfeet Nation is anxious to find an owner," Ellen said.

"Do you know anything about the haunting?" Tanya asked. "Is it one ghost or multiple? What have you heard?"

"It's not good," Sue said. "I wish I could say that no one died there."

Ellen glanced at Tanya, whose brows had lifted and whose jaw had dropped open.

"Why are you just now telling me this?" Tanya wanted to know.

"You know the answer to that question," Sue said, avoiding their gaze.

Tanya's face turned red, and she closed her mouth, her lips forming a straight line.

"Give her a chance to explain," Ellen said to Tanya, but Tanya said nothing in reply.

Sue leaned across the aisle with a hand on Ellen's armrest. "Well, according to the tribal secretary, the house was occupied by six different owners—all Blackfeet except for the most recent owner. The house was built in 1890 by its first owner and namesake, Talks to Buffalo. He and his wife lived there until they died—he around 1930 and she sometime in the early forties. The house was sold to another Blackfeet family with two children—a son and a daughter. They later claimed their son was possessed by an evil spirit for three or four years before it eventually took him one night in his sleep."

Tanya's face paled. "Unbelievable."

Ellen turned to Sue. "You should have told her."

"I tried to talk to both of you about the house," Sue said, "but you shut me down every time."

"That was before we agreed to come along," Ellen said. "You should have told us after we agreed but before we committed—before we got on this train."

"Are you saying you want to turn around and go home?" Sue asked.

Ellen glanced at Tanya, whose back was to her as she stared out the window at the passing buildings in downtown San Antonio.

Ellen said, "They won't stop the train. We'd have to wait to get off in Dallas."

Tanya turned to look at her. "Is that what you want?"

Ellen bit her bottom lip and shook her head. "We've been through this kind of thing before, and we're stronger for it. *You're* stronger for it."

Tanya wiped her eyes. "*Am* I?"

"Yes," Ellen said. "But we'll understand if you want to get off and turn around."

"I would have liked the choice before *now*."

"I know. I'm sorry."

Sue leaned across the aisle again. "*I'm* the one who's sorry, Tanya. Truly. I should have told you. I just really wanted you to come, because…" Sue broke down into tears. "Well, because it wouldn't be the same without you."

Tanya said nothing for several seconds before Ellen asked her, "What are you going to do?"

"I don't know yet. I guess I have a lot of time to think about it. Sue may as well tell us the rest of what she knows."

Sue dried her eyes and collected herself before continuing her story. "Okay. Let's see. After Talks to Buffalo and his wife, and then the family with the son who died, there was a family who lived there in the early fifties. Something similar happened to their son, only he didn't die. They moved away, off the reservation, to live with friends in another state, where they got medical treatment for the boy."

"That's a relief," Ellen said.

"A couple without any children occupied the house from 1954 through 1960. They reported years of harassment—furniture being rearranged, cabinets and drawers being opened, clothes pulled from their hangers, and stuff like that."

"No possession?" Ellen asked.

Sue shook her head. "But after six years, they were tired of it and moved. The fifth family had two sons, and both boys suffered and nearly died before the family moved in the late sixties."

Tanya shuddered. "Geez."

"The most recent owner was a single man in his forties, I think," Sue said. "He lived there until he died of a heart attack in 1973. He had no living relatives or close friends, so no one knows if he ever experienced anything unusual, or if his death was anything more than a regular heart attack."

"Hopefully, that's all it was," Ellen said.

"No one's occupied the house since 1973," Sue said. "The tribe has tried to sell it many times, but its reputation keeps potential buyers away. We're the first people to ask to look at the property in over ten years."

"Wow." Ellen could only imagine the condition the house must be in, to have been vacant for so long. "Does it have running water and electricity?"

"The tribal secretary wasn't sure when I asked," Sue replied. "But either way, this property is a steal. And from what I can tell using Google Earth, it has amazing views, not to mention its proximity to the park."

Ellen was glad they had decided to ship their equipment to Glacier Park Lodge rather than lug it around on the train. Spirits capable of possession and possibly murder would require every instrument and machine they had for a proper investigation. She'd been an emotional wreck for months and wasn't sure she was up for the challenge, but she refused to turn back, and she hoped Tanya would feel the same.

"I'll go with you to the park," Tanya finally said. "I'm dying to see it. But I don't know if I want to help with the paranormal investigation. I'll think about it."

"Thank you," Sue said. "Just having you along on the trip makes all the difference."

Ellen noticed the corners of Tanya's mouth lift into a barely perceptible smile.

"Sue's right," Ellen said. "You do what you feel comfortable doing. You don't need to step foot on the reservation."

"I do if we still plan to hit the casino," she said, her face back to its normal color.

"True," Ellen said with a laugh. "And we still plan to do that. Don't we, Sue?"

"Absolutely." Sue grinned. "Now, let's see about those margaritas!"

200

Eva Pohler is a *USA Today* bestselling author of over thirty novels in multiple genres, including mysteries, thrillers, and young adult paranormal romance based on Greek mythology. Her books have been described as "addictive" and "sure to thrill"—*Kirkus Reviews*.

To learn more about Eva and her books, and to sign up to hear about new releases, and sales, please visit her website at www.evapohler.com.

www.ingramcontent.com/pod-product-compliance
Lightning Source LLC
Chambersburg PA
CBHW061304210726
48293CB00003B/1103